MW01600974

Mudge & Where the Rainbow Ends

MUDGE & WHERE THE RAINBOW ENDS

FREDERICK BLANCH

ISBN: 978-1-942930-10-5

First Edition: February, 2015

Published by
Three Waters Publishing, LLC
Savage, Minnesota
http://threewaterspublishing.com

Printed and bound in the United States of America

Chapter Descriptions

DEDICATED

As always, to my two guardian angels

and to

the hundred and some librarians courageous
enough to have hosted my readings.

1

How it all Started

Frederick used t' say we growed up in more innocent times, "... when pictures didn't lie, an' when getting hitched could mean yer girlfriend's Pa could relax his trigger finger." But, even old ships keep sailin' on or sink, an' I understand drowning ain't fun – that's uh fancy, writin' way of sayin' times change, but lots of stuff don't.

Anyhow, Ah am writin' this here narrative to tributize my good friend, Frederick, who taught me most all Ah know about the writin' business, but now he's uh ex-author, an' uh former colleague, on account of he's went to the big library in the sky.

Anyhow, Ah'm gonna keep my promise an' honor his last re quest t' me.

"Mudge," he says, "I'm going to be starting a new chapter in the Big Book pretty soon . . . perhaps I should borrow from a Classic and say 'beneath the Couch of Earth Descend.' But, no matter how far I descend, I'd like to think my mentoring will count for something, and that you'll write your life story . . . the world needs farce and fiction, and outside of Washington, D C, you are its embodiment . . . just watch the run-on sentences."

Well, how could I say no after uh complimentation like that? Ah said, "You betcha . . . but . . . wheres ya headin' to?"

"Not . . . not sure, Mudge. Don't suppose the streets will be paved with gold, more likely brimstone."

Well, now he got t' talkin' on somethin' Ah knows uh thing er two about. Don't reckon Ah am familiar with what kinda stones them brims is, but the yellow stuff is, as they say, "right up mah alley."

Ah could tell he was serious about doin' his "Descend" thing on account of he started babbling about givin' someone the "Moving Finger" . . . an' ordinarily, he warn't that kinda fella.

"Write about those streets, Mudge . . . you've got the knack for it . . . write . . . just . . . jus . . ."

And then, bingo! Right there on the spot, Frederick's writin' part musta went looking for somethin' underneath that dirty "Couch," while the rest of 'im waited fer the undertaker.

———————◆———————

Frederick don't get all the credit fer turning me inta the pert-tin-A-shus writin' machine I become. Ah always been writin' somethin' er another, startin' after I learnt how t' operate uh crayola. Went through uh lotta crayons in them days an' writ up a storm in school, mostly on hallway walls, with uh fair amount of creative writin' on bus sides an' teachers' briefcases an' such. As Ah remembers, the hometown folks was pretty un edge-e-kated an' mostly didn't appreciate my literarian' ontah their stuff. Of course, then, Ah warn't the slick an' so-fisticated writer guy that Ah turned inta.

But now that Ah'm uh successful, big-time authorin' type, Ah'm gonna do like Frederick said, an' lay mah byography on to ya. So, here goes, Ah'm gonna recapitu-late, which is better than never, plum from the beginning.

2

NEW BOONIES, uH REAL PLACE

Mah own beginning begun in New Boonies, Minni-Soota, uh place where Ah come from. It's stuck into my heart tighter than the fishbone what choked Uncle Dibbly at the last Thudmunson/Wigglesword family reunion picnic, an' Ah ain't ashamed to say it's my hometown too.

But, of course, Ah gotta X-plane how it got to be a place, in the first place.

Back B-four the Civilian War, when uh lotta Southern folks wanted to succeed from the U. S. of A., an' A. Lincoln (the five dollar bill guy) threatened aggression on um, great, great Granddad, Lemuel Thudmunson, figured he'd git hisself outta the middle of that argument afore their disputin' turned t' shootin'. Anyhow, that was the o-fish-shill family story; actually, I guess he had to leave Ken-Tucky in uh hurry on account of he shot the mayor of Booneville in uh em-bare-ass-ing spot, right in the woods. Seems His Honor was re-leevin' hisself in uh brushy area, an' Lemuel, doing some deer hunting, fired at what he thought was a buck snortin' in the bushes. Figuring he owed Booneville something, g.g. Granddad named the hideaway he run to here in Minni-Soota (which might uh been uh Territory in them days), New Boonies.

Well, quicker than ya could say Jack Robinson, Lemuel got hisself married up with uh little lady from uh wagon train from Duluth, what was heading t' Ory-gone territory but warn't quite gone yet on account of they had stopped fer uh pee call by g.g. Grandad's tent, which was pitched right alongside of a favorite place fer wagon trains an' others to cross the Wet River – so much fer the hideaway plan. Anyhow, Lemuel went outside 'cause he thought it were raining an' this here little lady from Duluth caught his eye an' fergot to let it go. Turns out that great, great Grandma, the little lady from Duluth, also fergot to tell Lemuel she was already took into martro-money by a Duluth guy, name uh Jack Robinson. Of course, g.g. Granddad had to shoot Robinson an' that's how come he got uh limp – but that's another story. Over the years, quite uh passel of Thudmunsons an' Wiggleswords, from back in the hollers an' mountains where g. g. Granddad run from, come t' New Boonies on account of they figured the law might give uh feller more room here, uh few run off with uh new lady, an' sometimes, they come just fer uh change of scenery.

The little lady from Duluth kept pestering Lemuel to build a real log house with thick walls, so they could raise uh family proper like an' the neighbors wouldn't hear um so plain when they beat the kids. So, Lemuel traded uh slew of beaver skins to uh feller in Duluth fer uh saw an' that led to him building uh saw mill, right on the Wet River, which runs smack through New Boonies. Pretty soon, folks was coming from all over an' paying Lemuel to saw up boards, an' as Lemuel owned the only saw fer uh hunerd miles in any direction, he become uh big, important lumber bear on the Wet River.

Then Jimmy Jay Mound – the guy they named uh Mini Tropolis sub-herb after – run a railroad spur up to Lemuel's sawmill an' later, when them car-tog reefer fellas was making Minni-Soota's maps, they put in the places where the trains watered up, an' that's how New Boonies come to be a real place.

3

There Come uh Time

Every spring, New Boonies gits uh little water on Main Street, when the Wet River overflows.

But, years back, there come uh time when New Boonies got plum flooded all over from uh crime wave. Why, folks' washing got stole right off their clotheslines, outhouses was pushed over when it warn't even Halloween tipping season, and the J-walkin' from the Grand Saloon to Madam Sportains' Palace of Pleasure got downright dangerous. Main street was getting gridlocked an' most of the citizens agreed, *something haddah git dun to end the crime an' gridlock!*

The Mayor at the time, Cecil Thudmunson, nepotized New Boonies most expert fella on crime an' un-locking, which happened to be his own brother an' my great, great uncle, Plunder Thudmunson.

Not many folks was chummy with Plunder on account of he kept uh low profile (along with uh buncha other steel-tool files, fer his business, Jen U Wine Steal Tools). Plunder was uh feller ya didn't much want staying overnight at yer house on account of in the morning ya might wind up missing uh horse or the dinning room table – if the horse was strong enough. He was a sly one; ya could bet yer assets on that.

Great Uncle Plunder warn't much help solving the crime an' gridlock problem on account of he was busy watching to see what folks locked their doors an' after he got caught carrying away Padraig O'Murphy's washtub, Cecil resigned 'im from his un-gridlocking job, which probably wouldn't of happened, except Padraig O'Murphy complained so loud about it. Well, everbody knew Padraig was sort of uh bellyacher, but some said he had uh lee-jitty-mutt reason to complain about the washtub theft, seeing that, at the time, Mrs. O'Murphy was in the washtub.

Then uh whispering campaign about nepotism got to where it was out-loud talking an' g. g. Uncle Cecil was sorta steered into appointing uh committee of upstanding citizens to study on the matter. The committee decided that crime an' grid unlocking was a pretty tricky problem an' maybe New Boonies oughta hire uh o-fish-shill sheriff to handle it.

They got wind of uh wild-west-type fella (an' his sidekick) from uh newspaper brung in by uh salesman selling tin pie plates, which some years before he was probably peddling as gold panning equipment. Anyhow, uh gunslinger, name uh Boom Boom Blamberger, had uh ad-vertize-mint in the *San Jose Weekly Visitor* what said he was looking fer a sheriffin' job "back east" paying at least 10 dollars uh month, fer hisself an' his deputy, Lefaucheux, who, according to the ad, took out the "entire Jesse John Jackson stage coach robbing gang."

Figuring to git a whole police force, uh sheriff an' uh tough Frenchman, fer only 10 dollars uh month, the Mayor sent uh deli-gay-shun up to the schoolmarm at Huns Point to git a letter writ by her to offer the sheriffin' job to Mr. Blamberger an' his sidekick, Lefaucheux. Turned out the "Frenchman" was a 10 gauge, pinfire shotgun what cleared out the new Boonies crime an' gridlock in a hurry.

It's funny how Great Uncle Plunder worked his way back into this story. Uh couple of years after most of the crime an' that Main Street gridlock got busted up, Sheriff Blamberger caught Plunder breaking into the New Boonies Bottle & Billiards Club. Boom Boom turned both barrels loose an' that 10 gauge deputy unmortalized 'im, right on the spot. Actually, that spot was about all that was left of poor

6

old Uncle Plunder.

Of course, as I recalls the story, it saved quite a heap on buryin' expenses.

4

GENESIS 9:7 "... BE YE FRUITFUL..."

Soon after starting up his sawmill, g. g. Granddad Thudmunson visited Duluth to git his saw blade sharpened. Hear tell, he felt so bad after over-enjoying them Duluth drinking e-stab-lush-mints, that he dragged hisself into uh church on Sunday morning, just as the Preacher give a sermon on Genesis 9:7. Anyhow, that was the family story of why he fathered 16 kids, which kin make plenty of noise to git through them thick walls – but in them days, there warn't no neighbors to hear kids gitting beat, anyways. However, as time kept piling up sawdust, an' g.g. Grandpa kept uh sawin' and uh multiplyin', other folks moved into New Boonies so they could work in the sawmill an stuff, an' before ya could say Jack Robinson – is dead, g.g. Granddad's hideaway become a lively, bustling place (an' not because the ladies wore um at the time, but on account of it was busy too). It got so busy that Saturday nights on Main Street warn't uh safe place fer dogs t' sleep no more.

Actually, g.g. Granddad sort of made his own community, as his 15 boys growed up an' gradually took all the sawmill jobs, an' while they was at it, took most of the local ladies into the condition of matra-money, depending on how much pre-matra moanin' they done about their condition.

His only girl, Little Lady Junior, married up with uh poor boy, Sam Wigglesword, what worked in Lemuel's sawmill sawing with uh handsaw. Lemuel's sons would of probably forced him out too except he was uh workin' fool, an' made the sawmill uh lotta money. An' hear tell, he was about the nicest guy in Wet County, and it turned out that Little Lady Junior adored him – all of which probably meant nothing to the Thudmunson boys. They kept him on account of his arm muscles was big around as water buckets an' they was terrified of 'im.

Seems he shared old Lemuel's talent fer creating things an' over the years, he become uh guy what owned his own farm, right there on the edge of town, and had a dozen kids calling him Pa. An' that's how come the Wiggleswords an' Thudmunsons got to swappin' DNA, to the point it got hard to tell between um, just that New Boonies got uh lot of um. Practically everbody could of had one of them high phony-ated names but, in them days, folks didn't bother much with that kinda fancy stuff. New Boonians what warn't aunts or uncles of each other was bound to be cousins er nieces er nephews; we was whatcha might call inn-t-greated, one big happy family.

Of course, like any family, happy or whatever, New Boonies had its share uh whatever.

5

A Little Whatever Wanders Wherever

When Cousin Thudmore Wigglesword got rich, he couldn't keep no skeleton in the henhouse no more; seems money's gotta way of a-trackting a-tension. His wife, Gretta, went up to Huns Point an' inn-gauged uh fancy lawyerin' outfit what laid uh buncha D-vorce papers on 'im, accusin' 'im of hanky an' panky, an' whatever, with uh un-i-dent-t-fied female, now D-ceased, at whatever time past. Of course, they didn't say it as good as I just done. But, no matter how it got said, it were a handsome mouthful of ak-u-za-shuns.

It all started when his crazy cow Bessie decided that she were uh chicken.

Up to that time, Thudmore was poor as uh dormouse an' fighting to keep Bessie from breaking into the henhouse to sit on uh clutch of eggs. But it were uh loosing fight; the durn cow kept bustin' out the henhouse door an' E-ventually Thudmore got to making so many doors he went into the business an' practically every henhouse in Wet County, an' fer miles around, had uh Thudmore door on their henhouse which is how Thudmore become rich. An' when uh big-time reporter from up t' Huns Point come sniffing around fer background material on Thudmore, he discovered the bones of uh D-ceased individual behind uh feed-barrel in Thudmore's henhouse.

Well, as they say, that was when the chicken droppin's hit the fan.

Thudmore got uh murder charge stuck on 'im, until he X-plained hisself in court, which got printed in the *Huns Point Herald*. He testefyed:

"It started as just a summer thing, or fling, or whatever. I met Edna, the bones in question, at the Grand Saloon, down at New Boonies, and, shorting up a long story, she came and lived in my henhouse. And wouldn't you know, we had an early fall blizzard and Bessie picked that night to bust into the henhouse again, taking out the door, and poor Edna froze to the barrel of chicken feed. For a week, I couldn't pry her loose and so I just give up trying. Then I figured it'd be simpler all around, if I just let her stay there. Over the years, she became a skeleton."

Well, hankyin' er pankyin' er whateverin' didn't seem to come to no good fer nobody.

Nowadays, Thudmore's back to being dormouse poor on account of nobody is buying his henhouse doors no more, an' ex-wife Gretta left town with uh chickenfeed salesman. An', to pay that fancy lawyerin' outfit their D-vorce fees, which warn't chickenfeed, Thudmore got ordered to sell Bessie. So, she most likely didn't come out so good neither, probably winding up in somebody's Big Mack.

6

GIVIN' THE FINGER T' SIN

Besides raising cain down to the Grand Saloon in New Boonies, what gits raised most in Wet County is hogs. An' when ya thinks hogs, well, corn is practically sin-non-e-mus with hogs. An' I can't help thinking back when corn an' sin got growed into uh big to-do in New Boonies.

Seems Thor Wigglesword's boy, Jacob, got accused of masterminding the dastardly deed of leading some younguns to smoking cornsilk behind O'Murphy's barn. Well, O'Murphy claimed his barn coulda been burnt down 'cause the kids had matches, but the real fire got started when uh I-tin-irate prechin' fella, Billy Good Book, sort of uh Johnny Apple Seed of righteous-ness, come to town just at that time an' riled up folks by wanting Jacob t' git sent to re-form school on account of smoking was a sin, an' Jacob should be made uh example of, fer leading his friends into a life of sin an' D-botch-ury.

The town was just about split down the middle fer sending Jacob to re-form school or just chalking off the matter as kids X-periminting, so fergit it.

Of course, the sheriff were all fer clapping the poor kid in the clink, claiming cornsilk was uh gateway drug. Billy Good Book latched onto that, amplifyin' it to the "gateway to per-dish-un."

Then, the Ladies Augzillery to The New Boonies Righteous

Shepherds Lodge got their 2 cents worth into the tussle, only to git countered by an o-fish-shill white-paper from the Shepherd's Exhaulted Secretary of General Membership, asserting the kids was only X-pier-e-minting. I s'pose they come on that conclusion on account of there wasn't uh Righteous Shepherd what hadn't smoked uh little cornsilk when he were uh boy, an' it didn't seem to hurt them none.

Well, there they was, neither side could git uh ad-vantage on the tother side; it were uh real Mexican standoff, though, at the time, the only Mexican near there run uh chile an' taco joint in Duluth. The situation got to be knowed as the Great Corn Silk Stale Mate. But, just like most stuff, it got fergot when somebody fingered Billy Good Book as uh few-ja-tive from justice, an' he left town. Rumor was, the Huns Point cops got a warrant to pick him up fer disturbing the peace up there.

I guess sin D-siding ain't so easy on account of it's hard to put yer finger on what to D-side that sin is. S'pose it's up to whoever made the rules that morning.

7

Sometimes, Bare Facts Ain't Enough

I still got me the Newspaper headline from the *Huns Point Herald*: "Judge Rebuffs Both Parties." Ah keeps it folded in my wallet, to remind me that the writin' business kin be sort of fun while still being fill-uh-sop-ickul. That little article is about the commotion what went on in New Boonies when some big city characters wanted to run around in the woods just west of Cousin Frumkin's lower pasture, without no clothes on. All legal-like, they went to New Boonies City Hall an' got uh license to "cavort in-the-buff." They was restricted from coming closer than "six hundred feet from schools or churches" – which New Boonies didn't have none of at the time on account of folks got their learnin' in the schoolhouse up to Huns Point an' did most of their praying in the German Lutheran Church out by Wet Lake. They also had to agree to stay at least uh thousand feet away from any establishment what served liquor, of which there was several in New Boonies.

Well, them in-the-buff folks lived up to their license and kept their distance when cavortin', but the customers in the New Boonies drinking e-stab-lush-mints didn't sign no license about keeping no distance away from nobody, an ya kin sorta guess the con-c-quences of that! An' if that warn't enough trouble, the Ladies Augzillery to The New Boonies Righteous Shepherds Lodge got riled when the Shepherds appointed uh committee to study the problem, in de-tail.

Seems their husbands kept coming home from Lodge meetings with black eyes and various con-tuzh-uns on account of they all wanted to git on that Studying Committee, an' the competition fer committee service got uh mite con-tench-us. That just shows ya how community dead-e-kated an' righteous them Lodge fellers was.

Anyway, there seemed to be uh fair amount of disagreeing between the Ladies Augzillery to The New Boonies Righteous Shepherds Lodge and the Lodge members theyselves, on how much studying was necessary to identify the problem uh the bar patrons closin' the distance to them with no clothes. Most of the Studying Committee figured only uh hands-on investigation would adduce (there's one uh them big writin' words Frederick learned me) a final solution – of course, that was uh while before "final solution" got such a bad name. On the other hand, most uh the Ladies Augzillery thought uh hands-off policy was man-day-tory – or else! Finally, the Ladies Augzillery went to court an' got a temporary in-junction on the cavortin' folks who was obliged to cover up some of the bones uh contention – along with some of their skin. That got the cavortin' folks worked up into uh real sweat over havin' to put on clothing. They was so angry, they counter sued fer breech uh licentiousness on account of they had a valid license from City Hall.

Well, when the case finally come to court for a rez-o-lu-shun, believe me, scant attention got paid to the Exhibit Bs, but plenty on the Exhibit As. It ended up the jury couldn't D-cide and got hung – which both sides wanted to do to um anyway – an' the Judge had to do the D-cidin'.

The Judge banged his gavel. "Everybody go home," he said, "both cases are hereby dismissed."

Far as I know, them bare-naked bodies is still cavortin' around out in the woods west uh Frumkin's lower pasture, an' like the paper's headline, that Sol-O'man like Judge rebuffed everbody with a single stroke of his pen. Simultaneous like, when he rebuffed the Ladies Augszillery lawsuit, he re buffed them cavortin' folks.

16

8

Turkey for Thanksgiving

Ah knows Ahm uh curmudgeon, but Ah still feels uh mite vexed when holding uh door open fer uh body what breezes through without even no ack-knowledge-mint. Just uh smile or nod would do, but some folks is so busy thinking on their own stuff, they don't got time fer curt-essy, let alone being grateful. Of course, it ain't just uh city thing though, folks up to New Boonies kin be just as ungrateful as anybody. An' not appreciating uh favor reminds me of a story what was the Mother of un-great-full, what I got told in the New Boonies Tricho Treats. I know that's sort of uh P-cule-liar name fer uh barber shop, but it's run by Silas Syllable, uh fella what got a dictionary fer his twelfth birthday, what's on October 31st.

Seems out to the Manley Crum farm, they had a sow what throwed a runt in uh litter of prize pigs. Warn't all that unusual, but this runt had stripes running from head to twirley tail. It was so cute, they kept it as uh pet an' playmate for their four year old daughter, Blessed Angel. She got named that on account of Dorine an' Manley was in their fifties without nobody to in-hair-it the place, when Dorine got into the family way an' throwed um that sweet little girl.

Anyway, that piglet come to be uh real pal to Blessed Angel, her only other playmate besides uh Turkey named Trumpet. Well, as good luck would have it, Trumpet an' the piglet hit it off an' become friends, close as two pees in uh piddle, so much so that Blessed Angel named the little piglet, Turkey. Which was a good thing to remind her of her friend, Trumpet, on account of that Thanksgiving, Trumpet played a solo part on the dinner menu. That left Blessed Angel with just one pal an' she put up such a fuss on wanting Turkey to sleep in the house that Manley an' Dorine give in, even though the neighbors snickered about the Crums keeping uh pig as houseguest. But it were Manley took the most heat fer it, like when folks would say, "Howdy, Manley, how are things in the sty?" He'd grit his teeth an' smile, but Ahm sure he didn't like to be nobody's butt, of uh joke.

According to the story, Blessed Angel an' Turkey went everwheres together an' it were sort of amazing that the pig was house broke an' would fetch stuff, just like uh dog. Even Dorine stuck up fer having uh two hundred pound pig in the house, but Manley was worried that Turkey might get vicious on account of he never got newturd.

Well, it were just before Thanksgiving when kindling setting on the wood stove (which Dorine recalled leaving there) caught fire in the middle uh the night; the old lumber farmhouse went up like uh tinderbox. Dorine an' Manley made it out OK, but were near stricken when they thought Blessed Angel got took by the blaze. Ya kin imagine their relief when they seen Turkey dragging Blessed Angel outta the smoky ruins. Their daughter had nothing more wrong than uh little coughing.

Uh week or so after Thanksgiving, Manley was in the barbershop an his friend, Ding Mathews come in. Of course, all the talk was about the fire.

I'd guess Ding hadda guilty conscience at not rushing out to Crum's place the moment he knowed they got hit by fire. Hear tell, he said to Manley, "Woulda brung ya out something t' eat, but at the last minute, my horse come up lame. But we felt real sorry for ya . . . everything burnt up an' all. I suppose you folks didn't have much fer Thanksgiving dinner?"

"We didn't suffer none," said Crum, "not many trimmings, but we had Turkey."

9

The Little Flocculator That Wasn't

I guess I don't blame her over much, we all got hore moans, so it warn't likely malicious, just a case of them hores moanin' so loud she couldn't hear the voice of reason. Which, practically everbody in New Boonies knowed by then an' echoed her mother who said, "He's uh shifty, subtrafugin' swine swindler, give him up."

"But Mom," she's re-phew-ted as saying, "I just can't resist his adorably gorgeous, wavy, graying hair, he so distinguished looking." An' then she done it.

Our Mayor, Melba Zwieback, run off with Wiggy Zilch.

Wiggy come to New Boonies from "out east" somewheres an' bought the Boonies Bacon Beaters, a pretty durn good hog-racing team. Some suspected he was one uh them "out-east-hustler" types an' worried he was gonna sell out to Lost Angels, California. An' the New Boonies o-fish-shills got to worrying on loosing the team and was talked into building a new racing facility with uh track an' even uh settling lagoon fer the hog waste.

Wiggy appeared before the City Council an' said, "I'll put in zilch" (which Wiggy said with a small letter z, but which the Council heard as uh capital letter Z), "money for a new track and a crystal hog barn; you folks will be responsible for all costs not paid for by me." Sounded reasonable, seeing as the Council supposed that only a waste pond was at issue. "I heartily recommend your plan," said The Mayor, "Mr. Zilch, please explain the city's 'investment' in detail."

"Yes ma'am," says Wiggy, all business-like. "Besides the crystal barn, you folks will install a biologically assisted flocculator which converts the soluble biodegradable organics in the influent to a biomass which is able to settle as a sludge – which really amounts to little more than a settling pond."

He didn't say nothing about the stink. But that stink was nothing compared to the one when folks got wind of their taxes going sky high to pay fer uh fancy project what smelled offal. An' to top them troubles, Ziggy got called before the City Council on account of they figured he wasn't paying his share and he asked um, "What are you whining about, you had every opportunity to read the contract that states our contribution would be zilch – which is distinctly written with a small letter z."

"That stinks," says Councilman O'Murphy.

"But not as bad as the durn pond. What can we do about fixing that, Mr. Zilch?"

"You're out of order and that's an improper question, Mr Thudmunson," said the Mayor. "What can we do about fixing that, Mr. Zilch?"

"What you folks need is machine flocculation. Get rid of the stinky stuff quick. I can take care of the entire process, machine and all, but I'll need the money up front."

Well, you guessed it. More taxes. More money to Wiggy, but no shiny new flocculator for the New Boonies manure lagoon. The team was already sold to Lost Angels, Wiggy and the flocculator money had ab-scoundreled to wherever, an' the Mayor was missing! Turned out that shifty, subtrafugin' swine swindler stuck New Boonies with enough fertilizer to raise Peru's next corn crop, which uh smart young man, Manfried Scheistermann, bought and then sold to Peru.

Hear tell, Ms. Zwieback left Wiggy on account of his "adorably gorgeous, wavy, graying hair" was really uh wig. But, even though they're forgiving folks, if ex-Mayor Melba Zwieback ever showed up in New Boonies again, she'd be toast.

10

SPECIAL THINGS

When Uncle Morton talked me into coming down to live in Mini Tropolis, which is right there across the river from St. Paul, Ah had some serious giving-stuff-up to do. Stuff like sleeping till noon, fishing all afternoon, an' windin' up the day – until closing time – at New Boonies finest im-bye-bing E-stab-lush-mint, the Grand Saloon. Of course, I was busy thinking about writin' an' stuff, all the time. But, onest I got my head around moving, I packed uh gunny sack, thrun it in the back seat of my Buick, alongside of Aunt Thudalia's going-away-gift, her precious Johnny Dieffenbachia, an' made uh last visit to the most special place what New Boonies got, the Town Rock. Was a place I wanted to remember, on account of it sorta wrapped up what was not so good, and what was very good about New Boonies.

I guess nobody never paid no attention to Charlie Wigglesword until New Boonies bought uh bus so's they could git all the kids up to school in Huns Point at one time. The City Council bought it off of uh scrap dealer what buyed it from Ophelia School District 44. Well, it didn't run so the Council sent Old Charlie Wigglesword, (called Old Charlie, ever since he was twenty) over to Ophelia to start the thing an' git it back to New Boonies. Turned out that Old Charlie was the only guy what could keep the wore-out rattletrap running, so he got the job of driving it forth an' back to Huns Point and parked it in his ramshackle barn, what was otherwise empty, except fer his old tractor.

Old Charlie never married up, an' he always had uh big dog trailing after him – an' no matter how many dogs come an' went, he called every one of um, Dan. He lived onna piece of the original Sam Wigglesword place, 40 acres of played-out farm overlooking the Wet River ford, right at the edge of town. Every year, he an' his rickety old Farmall® tractor worked away at trying to coax uh crop of corn or wheat or beans outta the stony soil, which mostly blossomed rocks. So, he hadda take on motor repairing to pay fer his taxes an' drinkin' money.

One of them rocks, which musta come up from China, was half the size of my Buick and, they say, Old Charlie an' his Farmall® busted uh couple sets of loggin' chains draggin it plum inta the middle of his driveway to the farmhouse, so he could cuss it every day. He was pretty good at cussin', even on the school bus. Gitting right down to it, folks thought he was plum X-centric. An' you know, folks being folks, they made fun of Old Charlie, called him the village idiot, or worse, an' funned him by calling his dog Old Dan.

But, kids being kids, they loved Old Charlie an his dog, what would ride by Old Charlie's feet on the bus an' just thump his tail, whether he got pet or pestered.

However, when it come to toting their kids around, lots of people sorta objected to the town simpleton doing it. First off, Old Charlie could cuss a mule wearing earmuffs into conniptions; his student riders loved it, but his language didn't please none uh their Mamas or Papas. Next, his hands was permanently black, durn near to the elbows. This come from working in motor grease all the time plus an unfriendly relationship with soap. An', though nobody ever proved it, many said it warn't just the cold weather made him take on more anti-freeze than the bus. But, the main reason parents was concerned was that New Boonies didn't have no bridge going over the river. That's on account of the bedrock, which in the New Boonies area, is sometimes real close to the surface or even at or above ground level. Main Street continues right across the river where there's solid rock underlying the river, not

24

covered by more than uh few inches of water. It's lots safer than uh bridge, X-cepting fer uh hole alongside the ford, which everybody in New Boonies knows to A-void, an' in the Spring, when the river's flooding. That hole ain't very deep, but ya drop uh wheel into it, yer stuck till ya gits pulled out. An' naturally, the ford's a durn-site cheaper than any bridge. Well, most of the parents of the thirty or so kids what rode the school bus worried Old Charlie might run the bus into that hole during the Spring floods so they got uh P-tish-shun started, an' before ya knowed it, he got replaced on the bus by a nice young man what wore uh clean shirt. But, Charlie gotta con-sole-a-shun; he was allowed to garage the bus an' keep it running.

Folks say it didn't take no psycho allah-gist t' see he was broke up over it. Every day he'd drive his tractor to the edge of his farm, an' just set an' watch the school bus fording the river. From time to time, he'd git so close to Main Street that he'd put out one of his black hands an let it slide along the bus's side that had been repainted t' say, New Boonies Educational Department. His old dog would git outta the big tool box, what sat on the tractor tow bar, an' stretch once in uh while, but Old Charlie sat on his tractor like uh statue.

Lots of winter snow and an unusual cold Spring delayed the annual snow melt, but when it come, on a burst of extra warm weather an' rain, it was fast an' ferocious. It might have been the first part of May when, stationed at his vigil that generally caused great merriment among the townspeople, crazy Old Charlie sat out in the rain an' watched the school bus as it was slowly maneuvered across the ford through plunging waters; the young man what wore uh clean shirt was a careful driver. However, the Wet was rising rapidly and the swirling waters, an inexorable battering ram, pushed the light, backend of the bus off the roadway, dropping the right hind wheel into the now treacherous hole. The driver attempted to accelerate, but the troll of misfortune held the rescued scrap heap in a death grip. The driver, his clean shirt soaked, opened his window and screamed for help, but the rain was a louder voice.

A gathering crowd stood on the bank, some in rain slickers, some in T-shirts, a few still in night cloths, all shouting impotent encouragement. No one could wade in to save the children; the furious waters would simply sweep them to a watery death. No boats were nearby as, at the ford, the Wet River generally was too shallow to sustain even a canoe. The torrents of both river and sky roared, not quite covering the screams of thirty terrified children, but enough to make one of them mime fellas outta the frantic driver, wildly gesticulatin' from a front window.

Suddenly, a man-made dissonance pierced the tumultuous din: "put, put, put," a beat up old Farmall® tractor chugged down Main Street, into the ever-rising cauldron. Over the rain and ever louder rushing water, Old Charlie could be heard. "Git back intah the blankety-blank bus and gun the blank outta it . . . an' don't stop fer a blankin' thing til yer in Huns Point."

The engine on the Educational Department's junk-yard fugitive whined and roared. Old Charlie and the Farmall® smashed into the buses' back end, propelling it from the shallow hole. The faded-orange vehicle lurched forward, engine roaring, and inched through the frantic torrent, up onto the road leading to Huns Point. Suddenly the jubilating crowd went silent. All could see Old Charlie was struggling to git off the tractor but seemed to be held there by something. An' he hadda knowed the front end of the tractor would drop into that pocket in the rocks, an' there'd be no gitting it out till the flood finished. An' there he was, like he was stuck onto the seat or something. An' all the time the rain was pouring, an' the violent river was rising, right up t' Old Charlie's neck, when Dan come racing down the bank an', starting from a little above where the trapped man was, jumped in an' got swirled out to his friend, now just trying to keep his nose above the water. In an instant, except for uh black arm momentarily reaching outta the watery race, Old Charlie an' Dan disappeared in uh roiling thunder of rushing waves.

The Wet River rose another foot by noon an', repeating its

Springtime ritual, flooded over Main Street a bit. A couple of days later, the Wet had lost its anger, to the point where Old Charlie was retrieved, Dan locked in his arms. The heroic old man's overall pants leg had tangled onto the end of the tractor's clutch pedal, dooming him to stay with his tractor.

Old Charlie had no wife or kids, and his sorta cousin Wilbur Thudmunson, who practiced morticianing in the back room of his wife's beauty shop, assumed the double duty of undertaker and burying kin. Wilbur was quoted as saying, "I laid them out together, and we buried them together. I think Old Charlie would have been blankety-blank pleased." The pair was interred in the little park that centered New Boonies an' the Wet County Highway Dept. brought in their big front-end loader and moved that huge rock from Old Charlie's place to cap the grave.

Before leaving my home town, I wanted to go there just one more time an' read the little bronze plaque what was a wonder of eloquence:

Charlie & Dan

1952

11

WHAT'S INNA NAME

After Uncle Morton gimme uh invite to come an' live in Mini Tropolis, which is right there across the river from St. Paul, it were uh fair while where Ah thought that mighta been uh miss-take. On the good side, there was heaps more drinkin' e-stab-lush-mints, which was real good, but on the bad side, my new bar buddies made uh lotta fun of my name, an' Ah didn't like that none.

Uncle Mort, he's real smart, an' he gimme some good add vice when he told me, "Don't tell anybody your name is Wigglesword, just give them a common name, like Smith or Jones."

Well, that worked like uh charm, no more funnin' me on my name. Though, maybe they wasn't funnin' as much as they was deaf, on account of they kept asking "what" or "which" when Ah told um my name is, Smithorjones. The name thing kinda reminded me of another name thing, when Ah still lived in New Boonies an' went fer schoolin' up to Huns Point.

We was gitting learned about the American Revulsion from Ing Land, back when they was polite about their warring and had tea parties an' such, when Miss Smallermann says, "You know, boys and girls, we have Revolutionary history right here in Huns Point."

Well, as they say, we was all ears.

"Years ago, The Hudson Buy Company had an outpost, right

here on the Wet River and a stockade was built to protect the trading post. In time, the English christened it His Majesty's Fort. And, as you know, this area was originally settled by Teutonic peoples and because of the peculiarities of British accent, the word Fort was eventually Germanized as Fahrt, f-a-h-r-t , and the protective bulwarks assumed the title: His Majesty's Fahrt. Of course, in some English speaking circles, this rather *gasartig* appellation seemed somewhat unsuitable and was therefore anglicized as His Majesty's Wart. But wart or not, the English soldiers often mistreated the indigenous populace, seizing foodstuffs and violating their women; the locals began to see red any time a soldier left the wart. As a result, popular anger erupted as a pitchfork brandishing, broadaxe wielding mob that took possession of the wart and were only expelled when the British sent an entire regiment to reclaim their property. However, neither English nor local peoples forgot that, at the point of cold steel, the 'Huns,' British slang for our local folk, captured and held the fort – fahrt – wart, forever after known as Huns Point.

Of course, after Miss Smallermann finished up her story, we was all mouth. But, I never did git an answer to my question about them two tonics. S'posen they was German, one of um hadda be Leinenkugels.

12

Uh Bottle of Friendship

Was talking with Uncle Morton the other day about Famous couples like Butch Cassidy an' the Sundance Kid, an' Bonnie an' Clyde, kinda wishing I hadda sidekick on account of I don't know nobody much down here excepting my drinkin' buddies, which ain't really buddies.

"Closeness is no guarantee of happiness or satisfaction," says Mort, "Some couples never achieve happiness, look at Romeo and Juliet or Pelléas and Mélisande."

Well, Romeo an' his girl friend don't count none; them folks was always stickin' each other with them sill etto things er shakin' spears at each other. An' Ah don't see what uh pail of E-us an' uh mellon stand got t' do with couples, but Mort, he's uh deep one, so I don't usually argue none. But this time I got 'im. I knowed of uh couple fellows up to New Boonies what was famous fer sticking together through thick an' thicker, an' seeing as Mort is from New Boonies too, he shoulda heard about um.

"How about the O'Murphy boys?" I says.

"What about um? Hear Cletus died a while back. Probably a relief for Grand Saloon patrons . . . don't have to worry about getting clobbered by an errant chair with their Leinenkugel."

We was sittin' in a booth at the Town Tavern, which, for me, has kinda took the place of the Grand Saloon.

One of The Sippin Singers, Misty, what's sweet on Mort, was sitting with us an' says, "Errant chairs sound exciting, they must be interesting boys."

"Not so interesting that you'd want them for a party."

"Oh now Morton," I says, "they wasn't all bad, at least they was loyal t' each other."

"I like loyalty, too," claims Misty. "Go ahead, Mudge, lets hear what makes them such lousy dinner guest material."

"Well, Cletus and Clyde O'Murphy was cousins, knowed for sticking together. But, one of the times they didn't, Clete went to Duluth by hisself and got into uh nickel an' dime poker game where he won hisself uh $20 bottle of Jameson Irish Whisky. Well, nobody ever knowed either of them boys t' let uh cork stay inna whisky bottle overlong, but for some reason, Cletus just couldn't bring hisself to open up that bottle. Ah understand it drove Clyde durn near crazy. Anyhow, time got itself swallowed up like cheap whisky at uh Irish picnic, an' the O'Murphy boys each got theyselves matro moneyed up, had families and countless good times fighting up to the Grand Saloon an' looking out for each other's back all that time. Clete, he named his first boy Clyde an' Clyde returned the honor with a son the name uh Cletus. I guess ya could say them O'Murphy boys was closer than two pees in uh piddle.

Eventually Cletus got real sick an' asked Clyde to keep watch on that Jameson on account his last wish was to have it sprinkled on his grave. Naturally, being close as brothers, Cletus asked Clyde to do the sprinkling.

They say that after Cletus passed, Clyde just sat an' stared at that bottle for days, wrestling with his conscience: drink the whisky, or keep his moral duty to his friend. An' after uh week of sleepless nights, along about sunrise, he an' his wife drove out to Cletus' grave an' Clyde sprinkled the whole bottle of Jameson onto the grave.

Of course, like usual, some folks warn't satisfied with how Clyde honored his friend's last wish an' said he shoulda never drank the bottle first."

13

Luck Walks in Many Shoes

My new drinkin' buddies down to Marg & Ritas ain't very respectful; Jim, he called me uh "hick," an' Slim "Wheel" Barrow referred t' New Boonies as uh "nowheres place." Naturally, I told um that ain't true, if it warn't fer Wet County country, we might be livin' in Dakotasota instead of Minni Soota (snooty folks calls it Minnesota; Frederick says I should too, but sometimes I slip).

"You kin just explain that, Mr. Know It All," says Slim, "if ya buy a round of Leinenkugals."

Well, of course I don't "know it all," but they do tells uh story about Wet County an' surroundings bein' his-store-ickly important in how Minnesota got named that way. After the Revulsion from Ing Land, seems one of the founding Papas got uh great idea t' git rich; he'd underwrite uh X-pa-dish-un to Unnamed Indian country an' collect rabbits what got them huge feet what's good fer running on top of the snow without sinking in. He was gonna cut off their feet an sell um fer snowshoes, figurin' he'd clear uh bundle.

He hires uh couple of explorer types an' their clerk to traipse off t' the middle of Chipeway Country t' git them rabbits. So, the in-trepid three, Mary Weather, Loomis (never got uh first name on him), and their clerk, set out on what's now the Great Lakes and landed in what's now Duluth.

After resting-up, at what's now Duluth, they traveled as far west as what's now Wet County an' got lost. They asked some Indians where they was an got told, *"many snowtas."* Well, their clerk records that they knowed that, on account of they was up t' their bum fiddles in the white stuff. An' that's where the clerk's journal leaves off until Mary famouses herself by becomin' one of them his-store-ickal foot notes, as the first woman X-plorer t' put her foot through a birch bark canoe. (Of course, she hadda unfair add vantage over all the other women what put uh foot through canoes on account of she had a clerk right there to make uh his-torical note about her foot.) It was one of them kneedless tradgidees on account Loomis warned her to remove her fancy shoes in the canoe: "Them spike heels is gonna gitchee goomied . . . go through birch bark, quicker un uh tomahawk through uh fat Frenchman's scalp," the clerk reported. Well, Mary didn't take no heed an got herself goomied on the way home, right in the middle of Lake Mish Again. Anyhow, her partner Loomis and their clerk got back with uh big load of rabbit legs, but uh spell of warm weather struck the east an' instead of sellin' them feets as snowshoes, that foundin' Papa showed uh mighty smart streak of entrepreneurin' an' made uh killin' selling the feet offen them misfortunate rabbits t' folks as luck charms. Of course he didn't mention t' nobody what kinda luck them rabbits got, but he blowed up uh real big story on how lucky Loomis and his clerk was on account of runnin' after them rabbits run um right outta the clutches of a band of Chipeways what was peeved about outside folks stealin' their rabbits.

But I'm die-gressin' uh mite from how Minnesota got its name. Some claims the name Minnesota come from uh Dakota word meaning "clear water," which nowadays is kinda hard t' find. Some say what them Indians really said was *many snowtas* but trans late-in folks couldn't find no English words fer "too durn much snow," so they settled on "clear water."

One way er the other, uh lot come outta that X-poe-dish-un up around New Boonies. Minnesota picked up uh name – even it were wrong – an' uh lotta folks wound up with rabbit's foots.

But, when it come t' namin' the little critters, "lucky" rabbits had uh kinda un-in-ten-shun-all I-row-knee, so that's why they is knowed as snowshoe rabbits. Now, who says New Boonies ain't nowheres?

14

Some Folks is Deeper un Others

If there's one Wigglesword that our clan is 'specially proud of, it's my Uncle Morton. He's one of them fellas with uh buncha smarts under his hat, but he don't make no showoff deal over it. He was twelve when he hitched uh ride onna manure truck an' took off fer wherever. That got him arrested as uh truant an' then he got schooled in the Huns Point House of Reclamation for Wayward Youth.

While there, he organized uh protest what turned into uh riot and he managed to escape. He musta learnt protesting pretty good on account of he been mostly doing that ever since. Now, he gotta real cushy job atta fancy college what gives him time to go marching and protesting and stuff. An' he's gotta business card with uh lotta big words, but Ah don't think none of um is nasty, so here it is:

T. Throckmorton Wigglesword
Paladin of the subjugated & oppressed,
marching for meritorious causes
reasonable rates for:
- innocent intimidations • inflammatory rhetoric
- benevolent bullying • non-lethal provocations
- agitating & incitement • simple harassment & hectoring
10% DISCOUNT ON ORDINARY RABBLE-ROUSING

Mort has always kinda looked out fer me on account of he an' Pa was close, like after their war.

The brothers come home from Viet Nam and went into the construction business together an' hit the jackpot when they got uh contract to build The Vehicular Safety Museum up to Huns Point. They was hurrying to finish up the footings when uh cement truck backed over Pa an' pretty well flattened him out; Ma passed soon after, some say of uh broke up heart. Uncle Morton told everbody that he was gonna give up manuelin' an' laborin', an use his head. Which, Ah suppose were smart on account of he didn't wanna git backed over like Pa. Anyway, he applied fer some fancy, free scholarship to a college what was looking fer Vets an' they took 'im an' he like went forever an' finally got graduated outta the place with a B.S., uh M.S., an' uh PhD.

With all his learnin' an' letterin' he got hisself uh big-shot job as uh perfessor over t' the college near the Mrs. Sippi River. The back of his business card says he's uh Adjunct Professor of Chimeric Theory at the College of Ratiocination and Philomathics. Can't say I knows what he does, but it sure sounds right up there.

Some uh my drinkin' buddies down to Marg & Rita's Place funned me on all them alph-uh-bets around Mort's schoolin'; Ahm not over good at figuring puzzles, but Ah mighta done this one. I sure know what BS means – ya can't listen to no poly-ticians fer more un 5 minutes till ya got that figured out. The MS ain't so easy, but it's kinda logical to think it might mean More of the Same. The danged PhD had me stumped fer uh long spell, but Rita, what brung some Lieinenkugels over while we was arguing on it, come up with uh idea. She said, "Must mean Piled higher an' Deeper."

That's Mort alright, he's uh deep one.

15

AGREEING CAN BE DISAGREEABLE

Aunt Thudalia sent me uh *Huns Point Herald;* I hope Mort didn't go an' blab t' her I been sorta missin' New Boonies. On the other hand, it mighta been she wanted me to see the r-tickle on the Dumbrysick twins on account of she had circled uh headline, *Dumbrysick's Duel,* with bright yellow marker.

Them Dumbrysick twins never agreed on nothing that I knowed of, except they never give up being kinda loudmouth citizens of Rumungry, or wherever it was they come from, even when they got naturized into the U S of A. They come over here with their parents, what was nice, hard workin' folks, but them twins was bad news from the minute they stepped outta the railcar. They picked uh fight with every kid in New Boonies, and roughed me up oncet too, but that was nothin' compared t' the knock-down drag-outs they had with each other. Them boys wuz just plain disagreeable. If one of um said it was cold out, the other'd complain about the heat. If one wanted t' stay home, the other wanted t' go out; they was just about nothin' them boys couldn't git into uh fight over.

About the only thing they seen eye t' eye on was their bragging that they was the only ones in town what was sit-E-zens in two different countries. "We'll be dual citizens to the day we die," they'd say, with one voice.

Far as I was concerned, they warn't much welcome anywheres, and they could stick that dual sit-E-zen stuff right back where it come from. I kin remember more un oncet, the sheriff had t' settle um down, especially after uh afternoon at the Grand Saloon. And then, just about the time I moved down here, right across the river from St. Paul there, Esmeralda come t' watressin' at the Grand and them boys got about the biggest behavior change ya ever seed. No more picking on folks or funnin' them what had a limp, no more bickering over who'd drive or the weather or nothin'! All on account of they was both trying to im press Esmeralda.

According to the r-tickle them "terrible twins" turned into "beatific brothers," who couldn't have agreed more: Esmeralda was the woman of their dreams.

Woulda liked t' have read the rest of the story, but it was continued on page 3, which Aunt Thudalia had wrapped corn fritters in, which I like mightily, an' I could only figure out uh word here an' there in the last few sentences. Seems them boys got to agreeing so much on each likin' Esmeralda, that they got inta a duel and shot each other dead. Wow! That's serious agreein'.

I guess that right to the end, they was duel sit-E-zens.

16

CEMENTIN' uH RELATIONSHIP

Me un Mort was sitting in the back booth, where we could git uh clear view of the Sippin' Singers finishing off their set. They finally got done an' Misty come over on her break an' brung a tray of Leinenkugels.

Ah guess Ah was complaining to Mort that the Mini Tropolis cops busted up the disagreements at Marg & Rita's before they ever got a good start an', while Ah was complaining about stuff, Ah mentioned that time, down here in Mini Tropolis, seemed kinda draggin' . . . whereas, up t' New Boonies uh fella could go fishing or hunting whenever the thought struck – assumin' the game wardens was checking on them durn lawbreakers over t' Wet Lake. An', most evenings, ya could count onna good scrap down t' the Grand Saloon – which the Sheriff let go on till everbody got enough tuckered, but still able t' walk over t' the jail peaceable like, fer a good night's sleep.

"Most of us look at the past pretty favorably, Mudge. . . . Know you're sort of bored right now, but give living here a little time; before you know it, you'll be just as happy here as you were in New Boonies. Perhaps a change of friends might help. . . . Don't think your new buddies at Marg & Rita's are much of a positive societal influence."

Didn't exactly git his drift, but Ah think it meant he wants me t' spend more time with him, down t' the Town Tavern.

"You can always come marching with me, Mudge . . . give you something constructive to do."

Ah just ain't the marchin' type, but didn't wanna hurt Morts feelin's, so Ah reminds 'im of my bad feet. "You remember that time Ah hadda git chipped outta the C-ment, Mort. . . . Feet's been pretty touchy fer marchin', ever since."

"Oh, gee," say Mort, "when you mention that, I think back and remember New Boonies living as a bit slower . . . some ways, maybe a little sweeter, . . . not that I'd ever want to go back! But that driveway incident is really dear to my heart."

"I got five minutes left on break, says Misty, let's hear what it takes to pluck your heart strings."

"Not my story. Let Mudge tell it. Go ahead, my boy, tell Misty how you got weak ankles."

"It were back when I was uh kid, musta been somewheres around 6 or 7, when uh big-time perfesser of child psycho lodgy retired from some fancy, She-Cahgo college inta New Boonies on account of he heard it were a swell place fer relaxin', and practically no traffic at all. He come t' town with uh rep-phew-ta-shun he got from writin' uh dozen er so books on raisin' up children; though, come t' find out, he didn't have none of his own. Anyhow, he writ *Children Need Love, Children Deserve Love, We Must Love Children,* an' uh pile more. An', according to the book reviewin' lady in the *Huns Point Herald,* each one of them books said all A-dults had uh duty t' love kids un-kun-dish-un-alley an' not t' give um no discipline."

"Don't see much connection to Mort's heart or your ankles, and I only got a couple minutes left," says Misty.

"OK, I'll hurry. Bunch of us kids was playin' tag by the perfesser's house an' had no idea he just had uh load of fresh C-ment poured inta uh low spot in his driveway. Me un Timmy Thudmunson run across that spot an' got stuck up over the top of our socks inta that durn C-ment. Well, the perfesser come runnin' outta his house shoutin' curses and not doin' much of uh good job of lovin' us kids there in his driveway. We was screaming and yellin' fer help, but that dadburned guy hollered, 'I'll teach you little brats about trespassing!' An' he went an' got a lawn chair an' sat all afternoon and that night by the driveway while we was stuck solid.

"I guess Aunt Thudalia, that's mah Great Aunt what kinda raised me up, just about went crazy when I didn't come home that night an' when she finally found us, she went home an' called the Sheriff; then she called uh plumber from up t' Huns Point an' he come down and brung some coal chisels to chip us out with.

"There was uh lotta excitement in town an they jailed the perfesser, but later on he got sent to a nut house down by Moose Lake. But all that was big folks' doin's back then. These days, I remembers it good on account of my ankles swells up an' ache some when it rains in the Spring.

"Aunt Thudalia still gotta couple of the perfesser's books, but she got plants settin' on um now."

"Gosh, what a creep!"

"You're right about that, Misty." Then Mort added, "Seems the Professor liked his children better in the abstract than in the concrete."

17

Good Company

Boy, Ah don't know what Ah'd do without Uncle Mort. Of course, he's re-sponsible fer me bein' down here in the first place, but he seed in uh hurry how much Ahm missing New Boonies. An' bar buddies down t' Marg & Rita's Place mostly don't fill the bill fer good friends – unless yer willing to pick up the bill. Anyway, Mort come to my apartment last night carrying a good-sized cardboard box with uh pillow case draped over it.

"Got some company for you, Mudge."

Well, I heard of folks jumping outta cakes an' such, but that box was way too small fer uh cake-jumper t' fit into. "Box looks too small fer even Tom's Thumb."

"Better than Tom Thumb, I've got Socrates in here."

"Gee, Mort . . . don't think no guy small enough t' fit that box could sock nobody."

Mort whips off the pillowcase like uh bullfighter wavin' one of them sissy-lookin' capes.

"Look there, Dr. Lehrenfalsch, Biology Department, retired and gave me his parrot. I'm giving him to you, Mudge, so you'll have a companion of sorts. His name is Socrates."

First thing the durn bird done was jump up an' perch on the edge of the box, an' starts talking uh blue streak: "Ontogeny recapitulates phylogeny . . . awk! Ontogeny recapitulates phylogeny."

"What's he saying, Mort . . . cussin' at us in foreigner talk?"

"Not by a long shot, Mudge, that's a biological aphorism . . . likely picked up from Professor Lehrenfalsch."

"Well, sure sounds like cussin' t' me."

"Don't be a dummy about it, Mudge; just take my word for it. And, if it'll make you any happier, my office's been right next to Dr. Lehrenfalsch's for the last 4 years, and I've never heard this bird utter an imprecation."

"You ain't doin' too much better un the bird here, Mort. . . . Some of them two-bit words sound kinda foul."

Our conversation on big words got ended quick on account of that parrot hops off the box, right onta my arm, and starts sayin', "Dummy, dummy . . . Dummy, dummy."

How could I not like them words of friendship?

"Welcome t' yer new home, birdy, uh . . . Socrates."

18

The Customer Is Always Jen U Wine

The night Mort brung 'im over, Socrates seemed happy to sleep in his cardboard box. But the next night, there warn't nothing t' sleep in – the durn bird had shredded up his box inta little pieces.

When Ah called Mort he said, "The bird needs sleeping quarters, get him a cage right away, so he gets used to one . . . old Lehrenfalsch had him sitting on a perch . . . was pretty messy."

"Where do Ah find uh cage big enough fer'im?"

"Start out at any pet store, Mudge, they'll probable know."

———◆———

"How big is your bird, Sir?"

Ah held my hands uh little more un uh couple feet apart.

"I'm afraid I can't help, we specialize in canaries," the fella snickered, "you need a stall."

"Ah can't do no stallin' on account of he needs uh proper cage right away. Got any ideas?"

"Not that I can repeat." He sorta laughed again.

"Can ya just tell me where t' go?"

"Love to, Sir, but we're supposed to be polite to our customers." This time the fella outright laughs an waves another sales fella t' come over. "This just isn't sporting," he whispers t' the new guy, "we got us a genuine rube." He turns t' me and says, "We've got a special on rare Artic chameleons, Sir, they turn bone white so the polar bears can't see them." An' then, fer some reason both them fellas started belly laughin'.

Was then Ah caught on. They was funnin' me. Well, Ah didn't have no time t' waste so Ah grabbed 'is shirt front an' shook um uh mite. "It's uh good thing Ah ain't my uncle Thudmore, you fun him, an he'd arrange them pretty teeth soz they was chompin' on yesterday's breakfast. Now, just tell me where Ah kin find a big cage fer mah parrot?" By that time the fella was white enough soz the polar bears wouldn't find him neither, and nice as pie, he scribbled out uh add-dress on the back of uh store envelope.

"Is . . . is there anything else I can do for you, Sir?"

"Yes-sir-re-Bob, ya can be uh little more respectful t' the next 'rube' what comes in here, 'jen U wine' er not."

19

LA CAGE AUX FOLLES, & NO FOLDING

The feller what gimme the adddress fer uh big cage was right on, an' when Ah found the place, there was uh sign sayin': La Cage – for Every Purpose. Was on uh corner in uh sort of rundown neighborhood over in St. Paul. An' the moment Ah stepped in on the creaky ol' wooden floor, with every kinda cage ya could imagine stacked up in dusty piles, Ah felt sorta comfortable . . . like bein' back home.

Uh ancient lookin' feller what had more wrinkles than uh slept-in bed, an didn't come much higher on me than mah belt buckle, come out from behind uh old glass-top counter what was filled with traps was smaller than my fist.

"Gee. Ya ain't gonna catch many buffalos in them things," Ah says, pointing to the case.

"Those are for moles, young man." His head took uh little dip an' he says, "Sampson du Fontaine at your service; how may I help you?"

Boy! Could he ever give ett-E-ket lessons t' the smart aleck at that last place.

"Ahm lookin' fer a cage . . . fer mah parrot, what's about this big." Ah showed 'im with mah hands.

"Look over here, Sir."

"Wow! Didn't think id be so durn big."

"It's been my experience that folks bring back many bird cages.

. . . They find their pet needs more room. And there's another nice feature to this cage . . . just fits a newspaper without any folding or fitting."

"Uh newspaper?"

"Certainly, Sir. A staple of any parrot cage."

"Oh, Ah ain't gonna staple 'im . . . not even gonna fold 'im."

Mr. du Fountaine sorta cocks his head, like he's thinking on what t' say next. "The newspaper is for your parrot's sanitary purposes."

Well, uh house don't have t' fall on me t' git things. All of uh sudden it come t' me what he was talking about. "Oh. Ah gottcha . . . newspaper's, fer sanitary purposes."

The nice old gentleman helps me carry the cage out t' the Buick an', though it don't fit good in the trunk, he gits a short piece of rope an' we tie the trunk lid down over it. "The rest," as Uncle Morton would say, "is history."

But, as far as Socrates an' his cage is concerned, it sure ain't the rest of the newspaper business.

20

Double Duty, News, & Dudu

Mini Tropolis got uh newspaper, the *Steer Trombone,* which, Ah think, was bought off some Texas city by uh musical millionaire. Of course, it ain't as good readin' as the *Huns Point Herald,* but Ah think they try real hard. Uncle Morton says they got the name just right on account they's "Full of bull and tooting their horn about it." S'pose he's just sour-grapin' uh mite on account of they don't print much on them goofy causes he's always marchin' fer. But they's got uh lotta good stuff goin' fer um, like real good comics, especially on that there Ed-E-tore-E-ul page where they tells ya what t' think, an' they's got where the movies is, an' their best part is just like Mr. du Fountaine said, it just fits Socrates' cage.

Was uh little worried that the parrot birdie wouldn't take t' his new home none but, bless his heart, he sashayed inta his cage like he'd lived there all his days. He hopped up t' the swing near the cage top an' begin swingin' an' screechin', "Dummy, dummy . . . dummy, dummy," then blobs uh big mess, which was uh mess age t' me t' get goin' on some sanitaryin' so Ah telephoned up the *Steer Trombone* an got us uh sub scrip-shun.

◆

Warn't more un uh couple of weeks after gittin' Socrates uh proper cage when Uncle Morton gimme uh phone call. Ah didn't feel like gabbin' fer long on account of mah finger hurt so bad it were hard t' think on what we was talkin' about. He called t' tell me he'd be outta town fer uh few days . . . was gonna go on uh marchin' cam pain against the power company in North Dakota.

"What they dun t' ya, Mort?"

"Nothing directly. But they need to take cognizance that their wind farm is maiming and killing hundreds of innocent birds."

"Well, them kinda cogs don't make no sense t' me neither, but I ain't the tek-nickel type.

An' besides, I gotta go, mah finger is killin' me."

"What's the matter with it?"

"Ah musta tied the string too tight."

"OK. Mudge, why did you tie a string on your finger?"

"T' remind me?"

"Of what?"

"T' sneak up on Socrates an' see what he's doin' in his cage."

"This, I have to hear. Why on earth would you do that, Mudge?"

"He's kinda pee-Q-liar . . . it always happens when I put fresh newspapers in fer 'im. He don't seem t' git um dirty right away, just goes an' sits on um . . . so I wanna remember t' kinda spy on him, see what he's doin.'"

"Great idea, Mudge. There's lots of call for parrot spying. . . . Maybe you can go full time with it."

"Good bye, Mort, have uh nice trip." Ah hangs up an' more er less says t' mahself, "If Mort warn't so durn smart, Ah'd think he were uh nut case." Well, that's all it took. Socrates jumped up on his swing and commenced uh racket like uh body never heard, screechin', "Nutcase! Nutcase!"

The birdie must be smarter than Ah thought!

54

21

DISSEMBLING DIEFFENBACHIA

When Ah left New Boonies, Aunt Thudalia gimme her prize Johnny Dieffenbachia . . . s'pose t' re mind me not t' fertgit about where I come from. Uh course, Ah wouldn't forgit nothin' about her on account of she gimme uh raisin' when mah real Mom passed on; Ah couldn't love her more, no matter how hard I tried. She seen me through uh pile of good times and uh fair passel uh misery, like measles an' six months of whooping cough, C-ment stickin' an' uh badger bite what got infected so bad the doctor told her it it might terminalize me right inta the grave. An' I ain't gonna mention the number of times she bailed me outta trouble fer uh scuffle er such, up t' the Grand, when I got older.

Anyhow, that big ol' plant was give t' her by her fee-on-say, Johnny Windsong, who went up t' Alaska to work in uh gold mine so they could git enough money t' marry up. But he never come back and Aunt Thudalia never got married; she musta made uh thousand cuttings off that Dieffenbachia on account everbody in Wet County musta been give one.

Auntie had about uh zillion of them durn plants in the house an' Ah probably spilled uh fair bunch. At no time, however, did she ever git cross about it except the time I fell inta the Johnny Plant, the original she got from Mr. Windsong. So I was plenty took back that she gimme her beloved Johhny Dieffenbachia when I left fer down here, in the big city. It took up practically the whole back seat of mah Buick and Ah had to buy uh special table t' set the durn thing on, here in the apartment, where it takes up space what could be used fer something practical, like uh TV. But, thinkin' how useless that durn green monster is, I remembered Mr. Scheistermann, New Boonies banker, sayin', "If you think on it, there's almost nothing ain't useful." An' he oughta know . . . made uh fortune sellin' hog manure t' Peru.

Then it struck me. The Dieffenbachia was perfect cover. So, each day fer uh week er so, Ah slid that junior jungle closer an' closer t' Socrates' cage, until finally it was close enough fer me t' peep through an' see what he was doin when he got clean papers put into his cage. An' then Ah discovered what he was doin'.

Nothin'. Just staring at the paper.

I moved Johnny Dieffenbachia back by the window. Aunt Thudalia would approve of that.

As fer Socrates, maybe he ain't so smart after all.

22

SMART... IN THE EYE OF THE BEHOLDER

Along about the time Ah moved the Johnny Dieffenbachia away from his cage, Socrates would git t' pouting and then, outta the blue, go onna screechin' binge. He'd jump up on his swing an' start uh squawkin', "Dummy, dummy. Awk, dummy, dummy," sometimes fer twenty minutes at uh stretch, then fall silent and sorta sulk fer as long as uh day.

Ah got worried and called Mort t' see if he got any add vice.

"Where you been hiding, stranger . . . ? Misty and I've missed you, to say nothing about Leinenkugel sales plunging at the Tavern."

Didn't tell 'im Ah'd been hidin' behind the Dieffenbachia, I just said, "Ah been nursemaidin' that confounded E-motional birdie ya gimme. An' I wanna know if you knows any vets what kin help with uh screechin' problem."

"Not right off, Mudge, but I'll check with the biology department . . . see if they know of a good bird vet."

"Ah'd be obliged. An' t' answer yer question, Ah even hate t' go grocery shoppin' on account Socrates seems so D-pressed when Ah leaves."

———◆———

Well, to make uh long story uh tad mini mized, Mort referred me to uh Dr. Avias Dovecote, uh vet what teaches birdology er something at the big U-knee-ver-city by St. Paul. After uh lotta palaver, which on my bill they called uh consultation, the doctor wanted t' keep Socrates fer an X-tended observation, and so I left 'im there fer uh couple of weeks.

When Ah come t' pick up mah parrot the Doc says, "You've got yourself a pretty smart bird, Mudge. Fact is, he's so smart he looks down on most people."

"You sayin' Ah should lower his cage down uh little?"

"No. Giving you a reason for his condition."

"Which is?"

"In a nutshell, Mudge, I'd say pomposity compounded by hauteur."

". . . Uh pompadour caused by . . . Hey, he don't wear no hats!"

"That's not exactly . . . What I said was, pomposity compounded by hauteur."

"They got uh anti biotic fer that?"

"Not for that. . . . There was, we'd cure the world."

"I didn't bring the world in here, Doc, just my parrot. . . . You can't do nothing for 'im?"

". . . Afraid not. In my opinion, like many caged creatures, he needs mental stimulation."

"Fer gosh sakes, Doc, he got me t' talk to all day."

The doctor didn't say nothing right away, just stared at me. Kinda funny how folks do that. Finally he says, "Get your parrot a TV, Mr. Wigglesword."

Could Socrates got smarts after all?

23

THE 3 Rs: DISCOVERIN', INFORMIN', & LEARNIN'

Ah really couldn't believe mah ears. Thought maybe them Leinenkugels me an' Mort put away last night was revengin' on me. I do remembers comin' home an puttin' clean papers inta Socrates' cage, cussin' 'im a little fer throwin' birdseed onta the floor, an' watching the weather report on TV just afore goin' t' bed.

But, crackies! There it went again! Was plum light out so Ah didn't think it were uh burglar; there's nothin' in the apartment worth stealin'. But sure sounded like somebody was whisperin' in the living room. Quiet as uh mouse on French silk pie, Ah picked up mah diamond-willow cane from the corner and peeked around the doorway to the living room. If it were uh burglar, uh couple of smart whams with that stout walkin' stick would settle his hash good, but there warn't uh soul there. Durn!

Must be hearin' things that ain't there. Guess Ah shoulda listened more careful t' Aunt Thudalia's scoldin' on the evils of drinkin' . . . could practically see uh unruly mob of Leinenkugels settin' off uh riot inside mah head . . . an' then I seem him. He didn't notice me none, but I seen him good. Sure as Ah is uh foot high, Socrates was readin' the newspaper I stuck inta his cage last night!

Well, ya coulda knocked me inta the middle of St. Paul with uh tail-feather. I was brung up t' believe birds was stupid an' couldn't read, but here was one doin' it in his cage, right in the middle of mah livin' room.

Ah was struck dumber un Lot's wife – after she got salty! An' then Socrates notices me. He hops up t' his swing and starts t' cacklin'. "Dunny, dummy! Awk, dummy, dummy!

I looked him right in his eye an' told 'im, "You ain't foolin' me no more, birdie, you kin read!"

His eye is mostly white, but Ah swear, the real faint yellowish tint got more yellowish an' he squawked, "No birdie, no birdie . . . Socrates! . . . Socrates!"

"OK, Socrates, ya kin read."

"Mudge is smart . . . Mudge is smart."

24

Mudge Is Smart!

Made sure Mort had got uh few Leinenkugels under his belt afore Ah mentiond that Ah found Socrates readin' on the newspaper. Shoulda knowed it woulda took more un Leinenkugels.

"I know Thuddy brought you up properly, Mudge . . . pretty sure you're not prevaricating. I do believe you're just mistaken . . . or exaggerating."

Well, I knowed I wasn't X-zadgeratin' and I sneaked uh quick glance to mah lap an' didn't see no dark spots, so I didn't think I was havin' uh overflow problem er whatever the "pre . . . variation" thing was that Mort called it. "I ain't done none of them nasty things, Mort, I seen 'im readin', an' I heard 'im . . . words – an' – all!"

"I'm from Missouri on this one, Mudge . . . believe it when I see it. . . . Check that, I won't really believe he can read until I hear him do it. I'm free tomorrow evening, let's meet at your place, so I can see, and hear, this wonder first hand."

———◆———

Well, the readin' X-peer-E-mint were uh big fizzle, an' Uncle Morton thinks Ah gotta screw loose.

Fresh newspapers didn't help none, an' I pleaded with Socrates t' read fer Mort. But the durn parrot just swung on his swing and didn't read er say nothin'. We set there fer most three hours, until Mort finally says, "That does it, Mudge, your feathered friend is most undoubtedly a charlatan, a fake, or worse, a psychotic Psittacidea. . . ."

"Them's big bad words fer uh little birdie."

"OK, Mudge, he probably sat for too many years on old Lehrenfalsch's perch. In words you might like, he's bananas, an avian loony, don't let him make you into a nutcase too."

"Mort hardly got out the word "too" when Socrates starts swingin' violent like, an' screechin' at the top of his voice, "Nutcase! Nutcase! . . . Nutcase! Nutcase! . . . Mort's a nutcase!"

"Shut up! You manic moron," yelled Mort, but Socrates just drowned him out yellin' back,

"Nutcase! Nutcase! . . . Mort's a Nutcase! Nutcase!"

Mort stormed outta the apartment, yelling over the screamin' parrot, "Call me when you come to your senses."

The moment the door slammed shut, Socrates calmed down and in uh even voice, nice as pie says, "Mudge is smart . . . Mudge is smart."

25

Nutcase!

Ah felt real sad on account Ah s'posed Uncle Morton might be mad at me. I knowed he was truly mad at Socrates. Thought maybe he'd gimme uh call when Ah didn't show up at the Town Tavern fer uh couple of months there, but I didn't want to let nothin' come interfearin' with me an' Mort so on uh Thursday evening, which is solo night fer the Town Tavern Sippin' Singers, Ah stopped in t' say hello t' Mort. Well, Ah was more surprised than Rip van Winkle wakin' up t' miniskirts. On the other hand, was pleased as punch it weren't angryness kept Mort from callin' me fer so long.

Misty lays the news onta me that Mort's been in jail up in North Dakota, somethin' about marchin' without no permit. Guess Misty drove up there fer Mort's court date. She said, "90 days" rolled off the judge's tongue slicker un water offen uh greased duck's back – after uh witness told about Mort's skufflle with their local deputy

When Ah got home, Ah popped uh Leinenkugel. "Here's t' us, Mort."

"I know you're fond of 'nutcase,' you even babble about him when you're sleeping. . . . Personally, I can't stand him."

"Ohmahgosh!" I was so startled I coughed uh mouthful of brewski all over the Johnny Dieffenbachia.

"Who's here?" I demanded. But I couldn't see nobody. Was

about t' reach fer mah diamond-willow walkin' stick when I heard,

"Take the confounded sheet off the cage and you'll see!"

"You there, in mah parrot's cage, come on out afore Ah does ya some real D-bilitatin' bodily harm!"

"It's me, Mudge . . . Socrates."

"Dammies!" Didn't knowed if Ah'd had too many Leinenkugels . . . er maybe not enough. Anyhow, Ah jerked the cover offen the cage, t' see who was in there with mah parrot, but it were just Socrates. "But you can't talk like that!" I says, "You're a dumb animal!"

"Dumb? . . . Dumb? . . . A little like the pot calling the kettle black. Listen up, Mudge, I've got a thirty year college education, think you can match that?"

"No . . . no, but Ah made it clean through the eight grade . . . uh . . . high school took uh while."

"I rest my case."

"Well, Mr. Smarty, how come you wouldn't even read when Mort come over?"

"Because my world would get turned upside down if outsiders found out I could read. And imagine, for just a moment, how people would react if they found out I can talk conversationally. It's our little secret, Mudge, don't blow it."

"Maybe Ahm the nutcase, an' this just ain't happenin'."

"You're not, but you're sure related to one. Turn out the lights, Mudge, we'll talk about it in the morning."

I went to bed thinkin' that was uh powerful Leinenkugel. Or, maybe Ah'm uh jen U wine nutcase.

26

WEEDS

Aunt Thudalia used t' say, "Lies are like weeds, let one git uh start, an' they'll gobble up your garden." Didn't make uh lotta sense t' me then, but now, the meanin's kinda growin' on me.

We was in our favorite booth down t' the Town Tavern an' Mort was tellin' about his in-car-sir-A-shun up t' North Dakota, in uh "jail fit for homunculi . . . darn cell was so small you couldn't even change your mind till they let you out for exercise." Of course, Misty was sittin' next t' Mort an' she an him laughed like crazy. I was still tryin' t' re-member if Ah'd ever met that Hugh Monkuli fella – probably some I-talian marchin' buddy uh Mort's – so I missed the funny part.

But, I wasn't thinkin' on humor stuff; I truly wanted t' git things cleared up with Uncle Morton on account of the last time I seen um, he stormed outta my apartment madder than uh bull in fly season. Problem was, I couldn't tell 'im the truth about Socrates really readin', never mind the talking stuff. So, Ah let go uh big weed. Told Mort I was funnin' him about Socrates readin' the newspaper.

"I knew that, lad, but I do think you tried to carry the deception too far."

The second weed: "I apologize, Uncle Morton, sorry about tryin' t' hink ya."

"What's this all about?" asked Misty.

Third weed: "I was pullin Mort's leg uh while back, claimin' mah parrot could read."

"I'm surprised at you, Mudge, you ought to know Mort would never fall for a cockamamie fantasy like that." She turned t' Mort and run her hand through his hair. "My baby's way too smart to fall for that!"

Mort just smiled, but Ah could see that on his inside, he was sorta takin' uh big bow. Of course, it weren't long before I was plum overgrowed with weeds in mah "Socrates kin talk garden," and Ah been stuck with uh banner crop of um ever since.

Wasn't too long after that I gotta batch of corn fritters from Aunt Thudalia. As usual, they was wrapped in uh *Huns Point Herald*, this time with the O-bit-chew-airy Column circled in yellow marker. Well, mah heart done uh near somersault. Miss Smallermann done passed. She were mah teacher up t' Huns Point, an' I liked her truly; Ah used t' set in that schoolroom an' sometimes pretend she was mah Mom. Then Ah'd feel real guilty because Aunt Thudalia was the best Ma I coulda had.

Ever oncet in uh while, Aunt Thudalia used t' say, "My stars, Mudge, never saw a boy so durn set on gittin' t' school"; of course, Ah don't think she knowed how Ah was sorta stuck on Miss Smallermann.

Accordin' t' the o-bit-chew-airy there were uh visitation in the German Lutheran Church out t' Wet Lake. This was on account of Scotty Tavisher, the funeral fella up t' Huns Point, was still on suspension fer doin' some imitating. He got caught imitatin' uh joke they tells about uh more-tishun.

Ya know, the old story about the lady what viewed her husband, Herman, all laid out in the more-chew-airy. She complained he didn't look as good as the fellow in the casket next t' 'im, on account of that guy looked spiffy inna blue surge suit while Herman was gonna git buried in his brown corduroy.

The more-tish-un said, "No problem ma'am, we can fix that for ya, come in tomorrow morning for another look."

Next morning, there was Herman, all ready fer buryin' inuh snappy blue surge. Well, the lady were overcame with grati tooed. "Herman never looked so good; how can I ever thank you enough for all the trouble you must have gone to?"

"No trouble at all, ma'am," said the funeral director, "we just changed heads."

Well, Scotty put uh little twist on the story. Seems he kept uh couple uh bodies all dressed up, an' just stuck on the D-ceased heads fer viewin'. Then, on the way to the semi tary, he removed the body in the hearse, an' with the casket closed, nobody knowed it were just uh head gittin' buried; goodness knows how many times he used the same body. But nothin' good lasts forever, an' when all them weeds Scotty growed finally got uh trimmin', an' the sheriff finally gotta heads-up on that skullduggery, Scotty headed t' the Wet County jail fer six months an' his more-chew aryan license got suspend did fer uh year. An' that's how Miss Smallermann come t' git sent onward from the German Lutheran Church out by Wet Lake.

Seein' as I had uh real hankerin' t' see Miss Smallermann sent off, I asked Mort if he'd baby-sit Socrates while I went back up t' New Boonies fer uh couple of days. He didn't want to, big time, but when Ah X-plained it'd gimme uh chance t' visit Aunt Thudalia, which I was pinnin' t' do, he relented.

"But, Mudge, I hope you realize that caring for that blathering beast won't be one of my favorite pastimes."

Ah almost spilled the beans an' said I'd speak t' Socrates about his visitin' manners, but Ah caught mahself an' says, "Uh smart fella like you oughta figure uh way t' reckon with uh 'blathering beast.' " Another weed.

27

A Tear or Two

Ah never seen so many growed ups cryin' in one place before.

Near everbody I knowed in school showed up t' say goodbye t' Miss Smallermann. Turns out, Ah had uh fair bunch uh company thinkin' she were uh grand lady; the church couldn't hold near all the folks wantin' t' do their respects.

The preacher lamentin' her passin' commented on how Miss Smallermann didn't have much in this life, but he was sure she'd git uh lotta rewards in the next one. Ah looked around an' thought he was probably right, as long as all the love passin' between her and the folks here wishin' her well, didn't count fer nothin'. The preachin' went on an' on, becomin' like a music note, kinda like the wind blowin' through Uncle Harvey's corncrib, an' Ah got t' studying the ceiling trusses what looked mighty like them in O'Murphy's barn. An' suddenly, just poppin' inta mah head, Ah recollected hearin' Miss Smallermann talking about not flunkin' nobody in school; clear as uh bell, she was sayin', "You can't really go back, you have to go forward, to find what's at the end of your rainbow."

Uh slew uh cars an' pickups followed her up t' the Smallermann farm, a few miles northwest uh Huns Point, where she got lowered inta the company of her ancestors, in the family plot; they was most likely happy t' have such uh nice lady joinin' um. Mama Nature said goodbye, too; uh grouse in the nearby woods give uh drum roll salute. Her casket was lowered inta the ground an' uh lot of us threw uh flower er uh handful of dirt inta her restin' place. The crowd found their cars, an' then, I s'pose, most folks went back t' being busy with their own stuff.

Soon as the hearse pulls away, one of Miss Smallermann's nephews commences t' fill in her grave. There was somethin' kinda different about the peaceful little place an' it come t' me that there warn't no headstones like in regular semi tarys, just some mounds between half uh dozen big old oak trees. An' now Ah thinks on it, seems real fittin' for farmin' folk, monuments growin' outta the soil.

Drove back down t' New Boonies an' stayed overnight with Auntie. An' that was when she told me about Johnny. After supper, we got the fireplace uh goin' an' had us some hot cider with cinnamon sticks. Auntie's cat, Zingo, left her pillow fer uh spot by the fire, which added t' our cozy feelin'. An' there's somethin' peaceful about settin' in front of uh fire an' the twistin' an' turnin' of the flames what kinda pulls things from yer head that ya might not ordinarily think on.

I just suddenly blurted, "excuse words."

"What you say, dear?"

"Oh, just somethin'" popped inta mah mind. Miss Smallermann used t' say too many folks made uh habit of usin' 'excuse words.' "

"What'd she mean by that?"

"As Ah recollect, words makin' us look better'n we are, an' that."

"Well, like what?"

"Uh . . . stuff like sayin', 'Sorry, the rain made me late' . . . er, maybe, 'Ah can't pay ya on time, Ah thought there was more money in mah bank account.' She was kinda good at teachin' things on livin'. Uh course, she gimme uh hard time on some stuff . . . remember her sayin', 'Mudge, you, and come to think of it, most all the New Boonies children I've taught, seem to have your own language.' Then she'd laugh an' say, 'One of these days, maybe you'll slip a little Minnesotan into that Kentucky - Appalachian.' "

I don't think Aunt Thudalia noticed me wipin' up uh tear, but she said, "I know how you felt about your teacher, Mudge, you're sad she's gone, but you'll always have wonderful memories of her. . . . I know, I've lived on mine."

"Speakin' uh them memories, kin Ah ask ya uh real personal question."

"Of course, dear."

"How come ya never seemed interested in marryin'. . . . Was Ah in the way?"

"Oh, my darlin' boy! I can't describe how ya added t' my life . . . but your question . . . I never even thought of marriage. I'd given my heart to Johnny Windsong – forever. You remember that you and I used to pretty regularly drive out to Highland Corners? We'd sit by that little grove of popple trees for about ten minutes, just listening to um whisper . . . and you'd git so restless . . . remember?"

"Oh sure, out by them half-gone old Burma Shave signs. Hey, Ah remembers um,

" 'Don't take
"A curve'

"Then, two bent over sign posts where Charlie Neilberg went off the road the day of the Big Canada Howler blizzard. Then,

" 'A customer
"Burma Shave'

"Yeah, Ah sure remembers that spooky place, not a farm er soul in ten miles. What the heck were we doin' out there?"

"I was remembering."

"What?"

71

"Giving my heart to Johnny."

28

FROM TEARS TO TAPE

Didn't really think on it till Ah was drivin' back, but the couple of days in New Boonies didn't feel like Ah thought it would. It were nice, but it were uh visit. An' now Ah was headin' home, t' Mort an' Socrates, an' the hustle of the big city; I was bringin' back uh passel of memories an' uh big tin of corn fritters. But the surprisin' thing was that I knowed Ah was headin' home – "You can't really go back, you have to go forward . . ." an' I said it right out loud, "That's right Miss Smallermann, Ahm goin' home!"

Ah stopped by Uncle Morton's t' pick up Socrates an' he come t' the door lookin' like uh one-man war zone. "Crime-mah-netly! You been beat up?"

I seen Mort real mad before, sorta talks through his teeth an' he was doin' it now. "Don't want to talk about it, Mudge, just get your featherbrained friend and get him out of here."

I knowed he warn't anxious t' talk about whatever was botherin' 'im, so Ah asked how his Socrates sittin' worked out.

"Oh, fine, Mudge . . . perhaps the nadir of my life's experiences. Your beast is in that box." He pointed t' uh big cardboard carton settin' by the couch. "Take him home, now!" he shouted.

Well, Ah could see Mort was plum unsettled 'bout something, but couldn't figure out no reason fer his peevement. "Thanks fer watchin' 'im, Mort. . . . Say, yer bleedin' by that bandage on yer knuckles there, better git uh bigger Band-Aid®." Mort kinda gurgled, like he was sorta chokin' uh little but couldn't say nothin', he just holds the door open fer me. He's likely all choked up on account he's so glad t' see me, which is what makes homecomin' so nice. Double nice really, on account him bein' so otherwise grumpy an' all.

Thar warn't uh peep outta the carton, so Ah figure Socrates was sleepin'. Put him in the trunk real careful an' noticed the box was taped shut. S'pose Mort was makin' sure mah parrot was safe, so Ah D-sides t' wait till we gits home t' open it.

Jumpin' G-hoshaphat! Betcha I was heard clean t' the next block when I yelled, "What kinda nutcase done this to ya?" Coulda knocked me clean over by that pre-verb-E-al feather folks gits knocked over by, when ah opens up the carton an' found Socrates trussed up like . . . like . . . cain't think what he was trussed up like, but it was plenty good trussin' up! His feet was stuck together with uh stout rubber band, an' uh big mitten with the end cut off was pulled over his body so he couldn't stretch his wings none. But, the worst part of the trussin' up was his beak what was wound around with duct tape.

I got that durn tape off as gentle as I could an' washed the sticky stuff off with some vodka; all that time, Socrates didn't say nothin'.

"What in blue tarnation happened t' ya?"

"Forget it, Mudge, it's just one of those things."

"But . . ."

"Like Mort, I don't want to talk about it either . . . but you're right-on about 'nutcase.' "

———————◆———————

Mort didn't show at the Town Tavern for uh couple of weeks an' when he did, I asked him why he done such uh nasty thing t' mah parrot.

"The scatterbrained squawk-box drove me crazy, Mudge. The

more I told him to keep quiet, the more he screamed and yelled. The featherbrained fool finally went over the edge when he swung on my dinning room chandelier yelling, 'Mudge is smart, Mudge is smart.' "

I was dyin' t' tell how really smart Socrates was, but, of course, I'd give mah word t' Socrates t' not tell nobody. "He ain't no 'featherbrained fool,' Mort, he's uh pretty smart birdie."

If your bird is so darn smart, he knows a bag of rocks exceeds your perspicacity!"

"I don't know what sweatin' in the city got t' do with tapin' his beak shut, but you ain't never gonna baby-sit 'im again."

"You can take that to the bank, Mudge."

"Sometimes I don't follow Mort too good, an' Ah sure don't know how bankin' got inta our beak tapin' up con-ver-say-shun. He can be real deep; but sometimes, Ah think he's uh real deep nutcase.

29

LOST... IN TRANSLATION?

Me un Mort was kinda stood off from each other fer uh while after he taped up Socrates, but time, an' working together on reducin' the over supply of Leinenkugels, steered us back inta uh friendly rut. Ah was still uh mite shook that Uncle Morton would treat uh friend of mine with such mercilessness contempt-chew-ality, t' say nothin' about the brutalizin' part, but Mort seemed t' fergit all about it on account of he worried that Misty is actin' sorta strange an', Ah s'pose, his mind just natchural went t' his girlfriend.

Misty is the Soprano in the Sippin' Singers, the four ladies what sings backup t' most uh the guest pre formers, down t' the Town Tavern, and they sing solo on Thursday nights. Ah think Mort is uh lucky guy on account of Misty is uh real nice lady, an' Mort has got uh lotta unhappiness with past girlfriends, what in mah O-pinion, he is lucky they is past. But, now, it looks like he's havin' some sort of puzzlement with Misty.

It were uh Thursday evening an' the Singers was warblin' away like night an' gales when Mort says, "I'd like your take on something, Mudge. And, I don't mean to create a problem if none exists, but do you . . . notice anything . . . ah . . . different about Misty lately?"

"She sings like uh bird an' acts sweet on you as honey onna cracker, why?"

"Maybe she's working too hard, you know, memorizing all those songs and . . ."

"Hasn't she always done that?"

"That's what bothers me, Mudge . . . wondering if she's unhappy about . . . maybe about us."

"Ya mean me an' you?"

"No! I mean Misty and me! . . . She doesn't seem to look at me anymore!"

"Oh . . ." *Boy, fer Mort t' tell me something real personal . . . must be big serious.*

"Shussh . . . here she comes, now . . . not a breath of this . . . to anyone!"

Misty come over t' the booth an', just like regular, she's carryin' uh tray of brewskis. "Hi sweetie . . . hey, Mudge." She sets down by Mort but, by golly, she seems t' be lookin' fer somethin' out on the floor.

"What's new, Mis?"

"Nothin' much. How's your pet?"

Boy, Ah'll bet that's uh sore subject with Mort. "He's fine. . . . You sure sound good tonight. . . ."

Misty jumps up real quick. "Gotta go, boys, duty calls."

As we watched her go backstage, Ah had t' tell the truth. "Ah don't think it's just you she's not lookin at, Mort. Not oncest, when we was talkin', did she take her eyes off them folks on the floor out there. Ya think maybe she lost somethin'?"

30

Lester the Jester

Mort says he's kinda gittin' used to Misty watchin the floor. These days, she's doin' it even when she's singing, an' on top of that, Mort's seen her starin' at the floor behind the bar. He's trying t' jolly her outta her starin' by tellin' uh buncha jokes, t' take off her mind on it.

But jokes er no jokes, I know Uncle Morton's big-time worried about his girlfriend so, every Thursday evening, I turns on the TV fer Socrates, an' goes down t' the Town Tavern, like last Thursday. The Singers was finishin' up on uh song wantin' some roads out in the country t' take um home, an' Mort was in his favorite booth. Didn't get set fer much more than uh hello, when the singin' ends an' Misty come by.

"Hi guys," she spoke t' us, but was gazin' out on the floor, "got a spot for a girl to rest her throat?"

"You betcha, my dear," says Mort, "you rest yours, and we'll crank up ours. Say something funny, Mudge."

"Something funny Mudge. . . . But, I gotta tell ya, Mort, that don't sound special funny t' me. . . . Ya want real funny, yer too late . . . shoulda seen Lester the Jester, pre penny-ten-chury."

"If what I've heard is true, he was a very funny fellow . . . buddy of yours, wasn't he Mudge?"

"Sure was. Spent many uh afternoon hangin' out at the Grand with 'im . . . he were just as good as half uh dozen boilermakers, t' chase away the dulls. He always used t' say, "If uh guy can't laugh, he ain't got much."

"Isn't that the truth," says Misty, takin' her gaze offen the dance floor an glancin' at me.

Mort notices Misty's lapse uh floor-gazin' an quick like says, "Sounds like an interesting fellow, for sure . . . kind of a haunting story though. You were actually tangential to it. Right, Mudge?"

"As I recalls, Mort, it were too cloudy that day t' git uh tan, gentle er not . . . but Ah have always said, 'There but for Grace's God, went me.' "

As usual, Misty was bent on gittin' uh full story. "You can't leave it at that, Mudge, what about God, and Grace, and your friend . . . ah . . . Jester?"

Ah notices Misty was fergittin' the floor an' lookin' die wrecktly at me, so I knowed t' string the story out. "Was Lester, Lester the Jester, but tellin' 'bout him probably ull take uh couple uh Leinenkugels, . . ." Mort was smiling all over his face. ". . . Let's call Sally over an' git proper set to hear about little Lester Moore. . . ." Ah gotta add mitt, hadda wipe uh tear offen mah cheek afore speakin. ". . . Lester the Jester, uh real story-tellin' fella whose humorin' was downright funny.

"T' begin with, it were one of them times when Ah had me uh girlfriend, an' at that time, it were Grace Thudmunson; she were about uh fifty-seventh cousin but most of us in New Boonies was . . . matter of fact, Lester Moore was tech-nick-alley uh cousin by way of Camilla Holliway what married up with Hervey Wigglesword after Iris Thudmunson passed on. Anyhow, Grace an' me an' Lester was up t' the Grand Saloon one afternoon an' woulda got uh pretty good party goin' except I'd promised Grace I'd take her out t' the wedding re hearse ull of her friend, Thelma Thudmunson, at the German Lutheran Church out by Wet Lake.

"I really didn't wanna leave the Grand, but Grace says, 'I'm gonna git to the re hearsal, Mudge, come hell or high water. I wanna see Thelma married proper like, before my God and our friends, so you better keep your word.'

"Well, of course, I keep mah word, so me an' Grace left fer the re hearse ull an' Lester, hear tell, stayed fer uh while an' told funny stories t' some fishermen what had come t' throw uh line in the Wet. I guess they bought 'im brewskis as long as the jokes come out funny an' when Lester an' the fishermen got poured outta the Grand, Lester was in no shape t' drive. Of course, he wasn't in no shape t' walk neither, so he drives off an', wouldn'tcha know it, he went plum offen the road, drivin' in circles and doin' doughnuts all over Melton Steel III's soybean field, finally smashing right through Melton's barn door, bustin' it t' uh buncha of smithereens.

"Of all the barn doors Lester shoulda stayed away from smithereenin', it were Melton Steel's, on account of Melton's brother, Judge Harden Steel III, come from a long line of mean judges an' number III is the meanest Judge north of the E quator. Ah attended Lester's court A-peer-runce an' the first thing His Honor says is, 'You've got quite a reputation as a real jokester, Mr. Moore. Where's the humor in breaking a man's barn door into splinters?'

" 'If Ah was uh sea farin' man, Judge, Ahd say I busted that door inta barn-acles.'

"The folks in the courtroom did their share of bustin' – intah laughter. An' the Judge pounded his gavel, like t' make splinters outta his bench.

" 'Quiet! Quiet, or I'll hold the lot of you in contempt!' The courtroom uproarin' stopped in a hurry. 'Lester Moore, for driving while influenced by alcoholic spirits, for careless and negligent operation of a motor-vehicle, and for wanton and malicious destruction of property in excess of one thousand dollars, I sentence you to full financial restitution, costs incurred by this court of $500. . . .' His Honor give his brother, Melton, uh nod, then smirkin' at Lester's family an' friends, which was most of the folks present, says, '. . . And two years in state prison.'

"There was a sob, many gasped. Judge Steel's smirk come t' uh scowl. He turned to Lester an' said, 'Think you can laugh that off?'

"I visited Lester the first time when he'd been in the big lockup for about uh month. He was sorta happy, but he was plum stumped on one of the strange things that happened every night after lights-out. Seems he hears fellers whispering numbers er such an' then a lotta snickerin'. He don't know what's so funny, but bein' uh funny-type guy, he sure wanted t' find out. The mystery got solved by my second visit an' Lester was back t' his old jolly self. He found out what was goin' on, an' he had a funny project underway. Seems the inmates got all kinds of jokes memorized and then they numbered um. After lights-out, when there ain't supposed t' be any talkin', they just whispers out a number, easy to hear in the nighttime cellblock, an' the other fellers hear the number, think on the joke it represents, and everybody has a good laugh – even though it's uh real quiet laugh.

"Well, Lester told me that he brought uh passel of new jokes inta the prison an was busy spreadin' um t' his mates t' memorize an' git numbered. When I left that day, my friend was uh happy guy, thinkin' on how he was gonna im-press his new buddies.

"Next I heard, was the awful tragedy." I had t' stop an' take uh sip of Leinenkugel . . . was uh little thirsty an' some broke up.

"Don't stop now," says Misty.

"Yeah, go on, go on, " Mort chimes in.

"OK, OK. But from this point on, Ah don't know nothin' on it personally. Ah think his note give most of the reason. He spent more than uh year gittin' them new jokes spread around an' when it finally come t' where he could whisper out uh number, he said not uh single feller laughed . . . tried all his new jokes an' several of the regular ones – no laughs.

"Ya kin imagine what that done t' uh feller what got such uh hugh mung gus rep-phew-ta-shun fer funnyin' . . . name of Lester the Jester. An' when his cellmate told him not t' feel bad on account of "some folks just can't tell uh joke," well, that was too much fer uh Jester like Lester t' bear. That's when he twisted up uh bedsheet an' swung his-

82

self intah uh sue-uh-side, right there in his cell."

"How awful!" says Misty.

Of course, Ah couldn't figure out what Mort had t' say. "Sometimes funny is just truth dressed in jester's clothing."

Ah don't think what Lester was wearin' had nothin' t' do with his sue-uh-sidin'. An' there sure ain't nothin' funny about never bein' able t' hang around with Lester no more.

31

Uh Foot Ain't Necessarily 12 Inches

Give some folks an inch an' they takes uh mile, give other folks uh foot, an they might take it the wrong way, like Misty, Mort's girlfriend. Mort gimme uh call the other day an' wanted t' meet fer uh private conversation; we set uh time fer The Kaffe Kopp, uh coffee shop close t' my apartment.

I got there early an' got t' thinkin' on Grace Thudmunson who's married up nowadays, but we had real good times together. I sorta miss um but then I git t' thinkin' on Mort an' Misty an' Ah see maybe Ahm not so bad off. Then Mort comes in an' I know fer sure I don't miss no problems like he got with Misty.

"How's the coffee, Mudge?"

"It ain't Leinenkugel . . . but it's wet."

Mort looked at his watch an' says, "Hang in there, youngun, happy-hour's just around the corner. And, speaking of turning corners, I believe I've solved Misty's strange behavior, and I'm hoping you'll help me with an experiment."

"You outta know, Ahm always ready t' help ya, Mort. But, what ya got solved . . . she found what's she been lookin' for?"

"Don't think she's lost anything. I've been keeping notes, and after practically memorizing them, I've concluded that Misty is staring at peoples feet."

"You're joshin'!"

"Wish I were, Mudge. . . . No, I think Misty's developed a podophilia!"

"She ain't never been vaccinated?"

"Again, wish it were that easy. It's not communicable, it's a psychological condition."

"She gone mental on ya?"

"Not how I'd describe it, Mudge, and not for sure, certainly, but, in your terms, perhaps . . . a little. But that's where you come in . . . our little experiment."

"Whatcha want me t' do?"

"All you have to do is remove one shoe and your sock . . . when we're sharing a brew with Misty."

"Take off mah shoe? Sounds downright kinky to me, Mort!"

"I suppose you're right, but perhaps it will be the proverbial proof of the pudding."

"Don't git ya, Mort."

"You know, Mudge, 'the proof of the pudding is in the eating.' "

"Misty ain't gonna eat mah foot, is she?"

"Of course not, I simply want to observe her reaction to your bare foot. . . . I'll be right there, Mudge. What could go wrong?"

32

The Scheme Is Afoot

We was all set. Ah didn't wear no socks at all, an' me an' Mort had gone t' the shoe store an' bought me uh pair of loafers, which I could just slip off easy like. Durin' the Sippin' Singers break, Misty come t' our booth and, as usual, sits by Mort.

Uncle Morton winks, which was our secret signal, an' I slips off mah shoe an', on account of I was sittin' die-wreck-lee across from Misty, puts mah bare foot right on the seat beside her. That was the plan. Actually, I sorta missed the beside her part uh little bit, an' stuck mah foot smack intah the middle of her lap.

The idea of the X-peer-E-mint, accordin' t' Uncle Mort, was t' see what kinda reaction Misty would have. Dependin' on how she looked at mah foot, Mort was gonna D-cide if she was sufferin' from uh foot ish thing. Well, Misty give uh reaction all right, she grabs mah foot an' starts screamin' about gittin' A-salted an' A-tacked. Mah ankle durn near got broke when, still holdin' on t' it, she tries t' jump on top of the booth table, all the while screamin' at the top of her lungs, which is pretty good screamin' on account of her bein' uh singer an' all. Ever-body in the place come runnin' over t' see who was killin' who, an' uh off-duty cop come over an' swats me on the head with uh little black thing that was harder than uh brick. My head started bleedin' all over an' somebody yells, "The guy shot her!" and the whole place goes nuts when everbody tries t' git out through the door, all at one time.

Well, Ah don't want t' make uh big thing outta the in-C-dent, but the fire department come and chopped uh buncha holes intah the wall an' roof afore they found there wasn't no fire, an', I hear tell, the street out front got so clogged up with cop cars they hadda git uh couple uh tow-trucks t' git um un-tangled.

After bein' re strained in handcuffs the size of Leinenkugel kegs fer uh couple of hours, Ah hadda go intah the men's room an' drop mah breeches t' prove t' uh whole squad of D-teck-tives that mah violatin' an' assaultin' part would uh never reached from my side of the booth over t' Misty, who claimed she got "violated and assaulted" by me what had "gone berserk with a grotesquely oversized private part." An' that was plum M bare assin' on account of one uh them D-teck-tives says, "My gosh, fella, that wouldn't even reach t' your side of the booth."

Ah kinda lost track of Mort an' Misty on account of Ah was bleedin' an' had uh head what felt like that cop was still whalin' on it. Finally, the Tavern sort of cleared out an' uh cop what didn't have no little black thing gimme uh ride t' the hospital E-merge-gen-C room, where they stitched up mah head, an' gimme some pain pills. Ah hitched-hiked back t' the apartment which took uh bit of time seein' it were about 3:00 in the morning.

Next day, Ah don't think mah splittin' headache got intah the way of makin' uh decision, t' cut way back on X-peer-E-mintin'.

33

Too Hot to Handle

Was uh week before Mort calls an' gimme uh kinda apology fer things gittin' outta hand, er ya might say foot, with our X-peer-E-mint.

"Terribly sorry about your head, Mudge."

"Me too, Mort. If I'd hadda choice, I'd of took one looks like uh movie star. . . . How's your girlfriend?"

"Ah, good to hear the old sense of humor is back. . . . Misty's got a problem, but I think we've got a handle on things . . . professional help. Colleague of mine, Dr. Ogar Shaman has agreed to take her case. He hasn't seen her yet, but I understand he's working out a treatment strategy right now. I'm fairly optimistic . . . not all that serious to begin with . . . certainly a lot worse things out there."

"Sounds good, when are we gonna get together?"

"That's another . . . ah . . . issue, Mudge. Of course, I couldn't let on to Misty we were subjecting her to a . . . a test . . . so I . . . I had to throw you under the bus, as they say. Bottom line is, you and I have to kind of put things on hold . . . just for a while, till things get back to normal. . . ."

"Ya actually means, till Misty gits back t' normal."

"That's about the size of it, Mudge . . . and . . . uh . . . Town Tavern has banned you. I'm sure they'll come to their senses, but for a little while . . ."

"I understand, Mort, another bus."

"Yeah."

"Well, call me when Ah kin ride 'stead uh bein' pavement. . . . Bye."

I'm not sure if Mort said goodbye or not. Guess that's uh bridge sure got burnt up . . . but, like any burn, it hurts like crazy. At least he got me one good friend.

"Socrates, whatcha want on the TV tonight?"

34

History Sometimes Catches Up

It's funny how Mama Nature seems t' be one step ahead uh things. Ah was serious thinkin' on goin' back t' New Boonies fer awhile on account of Ah got t' wait out Misty gittin' her head fixed soz me an' Mort kin re zoom ridin' on top uh the bus together. Warn't more un uh couple uh days after Uncle Morton put the quits t' us that Aunt Thudalia calls an' asks me t' come back soz Ah kin take her up t' Huns Point.

Seein' as she usually don't go on trips t' nowheres real big like Duluth er Huns Point, I knowed this wasn't nothin' ordinary.

"Don't know why, Mudge dear, but I got a letter from a lawyer, Pilfer Thudmunson, you know, great nephew of that old fellow we tell the stories about, Plunder Thudmunson. . . ."

"Lawyer, uh? Sorta following in the family stealin' business. . . ."

"Be kind, sweetheart, don't pre-judge. Anyway, he said it concerned a matter of 'major importance' t' me. . . . What in the world do you suppose that could be?"

"I'll be up soon's Ah kin find uh new babysitter fer mah parrot. . . ."

"Doesn't Morton . . . ?"

"Mort's out. Tell ya all about that when I gits there."

Boy! Huns Point has gone real big city. Got places scrapin' the sky all uh the way up t' six stories, I know on account of I counted um! When I goed t' school, the bell tower fer startin' an' recess was the tallest thing in Huns Point . . . except Ah fergot, I think the grain elevator was uh little taller. An, lawyerin' must pay as good as burglarin'. Thudmunson & Kraut was on the top floor of the Point Professional Building an' was about the fanciest place I ever been. Me an' Aunt Thudalia sat an' waited in chairs with stuffin' inside um, and we noticed that the rugs went clean up t' the walls.

We was finally took inta another fancy room by uh lady what sat at uh desk where we waited.

She introduced us, real spiffy like, "Mr. Thudmunson, this is Thudalia Wigglesword and her son, Mudge." The lawyer was uh Thudmunson alright, six foot three or four, lots of chocolate brown hair, kinda skinny, with uh face needin' uh smile.

"Son?" The lawyer's voice went up with his eyebrows.

Ah saved him further wonderment. "Adopted," Ah says. That seemed to put everybody intah the proper pigeonhole fer 'im, an' along with the eyebrows, he settles right down.

"I come from you folks' territory, so in the interest of conviviality, just call me Pilpher." He give us uh big smile that quicker un ya could say Jack Robinson – got shot by great, great granddad Thudmunson – fell offen his face an' we got down t' business.

"Ms. Wigglesword, I have been appointed Minnesota fiduciary in the matter of a bequest to you. A Mr. Johnathon Windsong has bequeathed his interest in a cash account, jointly registered to Mr. Windsong and yourself, and a fifty percent interest in the Big Nugget Saloon. . . . It's in Alaska . . . Desperation, Alaska. Oh, and a large, sturdy shipping case secured in our vault, here in the basement.

Aunt Thadalia turned white as new snow in Alaska. "All these years . . . Johnny was alive?"

"Not sure I understand your meaning, Ms. Wigglesword."

"How long ago did Mr. Windsong die?" I asked.

"Ummm, let's see." The lawyer thumbed through papers in a yellowish file folder. ". . . Uh, yes, right here, was in May this year, these things take a while to process . . . I . . ."

"I . . . I don't want any of it!" Tears were rolling down Aunt Thudalia's cheeks. She fished into her purse and found a hanky which wetted up pretty quick.

"Surely, you're not serious, Ms. Wigglesword?"

Getting' her voice back to near OK, Auntie says, "I mean it! Not a nickel."

"But . . . but . . . your boy here . . . would miss out of his inheritance."

I wondered if maybe Pilpher would be missin' outta his fee er somethin'. He sure seemed awful set on lookin' out fer our welfare.

Aunt Thudalia took the handky away from her nose. "I . . . I hadn't thought of that. I still don't want any of it. If you can fix it to go to Mudge, fine, otherwise just send it back . . . if that's what you do."

An' that's how one day I was broke an' under uh bus, an' practically the next, I owned half uh saloon an' was on top of the world.

But, of course, it warn't quite that simple.

35

Startin' New Histories

First thing Ah done when I got home was go downstairs an' git Socrates from nice old Mr. Sicamon. He said it were a pleasure t' have the company of such "a nice mannered bird." Wish Mort coulda heard that. But I got so much t' do Ah ain't got much time t' worry about Mort.

Turned out there was enough in that bank account fer me t' buy uh house. Don't want nothin' fancy, just uh place I kin call uh home. After I get settled in, Ahm gonna make uh long distance telephone call all the way up to Desperation, Alaska an talk t' uh Dale Windsong, mah partner what's runnin' our saloon.

Ah couldn't of done none of this stuff without Mr. Thudmunson's help. Ahm A-shamed on account of Aunt Thudalia was plum right about mah pre-judgin', which learned me uh good lesson. Pilpher Thudmunson turned out t' be jen-U-wine interested in add-ministerin' the leg-uh-C left by Johnny Windsong, an' uh real nice guy t' me.

——————◆——————

Mah new neighbor what lives next door, MerryMae Hehm, brung over uh vegetable pie which she says is very healthful. She also says she ain't married, except to her work, which is fortune tellin'.

Her pie don't taste very good so Ah suppose it's real good fer ya, but Socrates won't eat none of it. Fer the sake uh her business, Ah hope she's better at fortune telling than pie makin'. When she left, she said, "Bring your parrot over to meet Chrys, I know he'd surely like the company." Ah said Ah would, on account of Socrates likes friendly folks, but Ah fergot t' ask if Chrys is her boy er girl; them double-duty names is confusin'.

Miss Hehm, that's the fortune tellin' lady what lives next door, turned out t' be right friendly, but ah think she got me pegged fer bein' uh mite bashful on social stuff.

"You gotta meet your neighbors, Mudge."

Well, good t' her word, she sprung uh git-to-know-folks-livin'-close-by shindig in her back yard, fried mighty tasty hamburgers onna little wire contraption over uh bowel of charcoal, an' set out some real good potato salad. Addin' t' the pleasure of the picnic was that she didn't make no vegetable pie. Ah had asked her if Ah could bring uh couple of friends, she said sure, soz I brung Socrates an' uh keg uh brewski.

Ah knowed I was unlikely t' remember everbody, so Ah snuck in uh pencil an' paper, an' when nobody was lookin', writ down their names. Uh old geezer, Samson Santé an' his wife Dolly, kept arguin' with uh elderly lady, uh Miss Millicent Foyle, about who had the most operations. I think Miss Foyle seemed t' steal the decrepit derby when she said she gotta whole bag of colly-S timmys, but Ah can't figure out what collies got t' do with her operations . . . except, when Ah was uh little kid, I did have uh collie named Timmy, what Aunt Thudalia got me.

There was uh nice couple, Sven Erik & Rundi Oleson, what had moved t' the neighborhood not long before me. They come from New Sweden township over t' Nicollet County and Rundi took second place at the Nicollet County Fair Quiltin' Contest last year down t' St. Peter, an' Sven's tryin' t' catch on with the County Highway D-partment as uh truck driver.

Uh skinny fella what stuffed in about uh dozen hamburgers didn't talk much. He come late an' was wearin' dark glasses. MerryMae gives him uh hard look, puts her forefinger up by an eye, an' kinda shakes her head. Like the guy gotta E-lectric shock he grabs off the shades and pockets um.

Don't know what it meant, but MerryMae kinda smiles and nods. Come t' find out, that was Pencil Fliddy, an A-count-ant what lives up the block.

Then there were Frederick. Never did git his last name. He were uh writer what didn't say much except he was writin' uh short story on fortune tellin'; he was there, he said, t' observe Ms. Hehm and Chrys. Ah asked him how he could tell when his story was short enough t' be done an' he says, "I write it, and if there's anything left after I edit out the balony, it's done."

Funny he mentioned Chrys, I ain't met – I'll be durned, don't know t' say him or her – yet.

36

Gender Specific

Boy! Mort would never believe that bus he thrun me under was like uh regular airplane Ahm riden' on top of. New house, new people t' know, an' now, the mailman brung me uh letter that warn't uh bill. It was from mah partner, up t' Alaska, an' it said,

Dear Mr. Wigglesword,

Just a few lines of introduction. As my late father has seen fit to add your mother, and through her you, to the Windsong family enterprise of many years, I feel it my duty, because he would have wished it so, to extend a welcome.

Our state-side attorney, Mr. Thudmunson, has informed me that you were adopted at an early age by Ms. Wigglesword, an acquaintance of Dad's. My mother died as I was born, and my father has been my only family all my life.

Therefore, please allow me to think of you as my lower 48 family. My only ventures outside consisted of schooling in California, but Minnesota sounds much more similar to my everyday

experience. I hope we may meet soon.

Regards,
Dale Windsong

Gosh, I wish Mort was here t' help me answer this on account of it sounds kinda smart. That's when I got me the idea of gittin' uh real writer t' make uh re ply, an' I thought uh the writin' guy I met at MerryMae's picnic behind her house.

When I went over t' mah neighbor's t' git the Frederick guy's phone number, I finally met Chrys. Wowee! Chrys ain't uh he er uh she er maybe ain't even uh it. Looks like uh ball of clear ice settin' onna little black stand what MerryMae says is made from real ebb bony wood. She says Chrys is pure crystal.

Well, MerryMae introduced me t' Chrys just like any person an' that knockin'-over-feather is gittin' plum wore out on account of, again, I coulda got knocked over by it; that there crystal ball turned from clear an' glowed uh nice light green.

MerryMae sounded like uh proud mother. "Oh, how wonderful, Chrys likes you, Mudge . . . see, he's green!"

Oh, I picked up on that "he." Of course, it figures, ball an' all.

"But right now," she says, "let's find that number . . . right here in my book. I'll do a little demonstration for you." She gits out uh address book from uh purse that's bigger than uh suitcase. "The writer, Frederick . . . what page, Chrys?"

The durn ball turned kinda brown an' I couldn't see nothin' but MerryMae sorta sings out, "Page 14 . . . let's see . . . right on, my lovely."

I swear the thing turned green again. Anyway I got the writer's phone number and after promisin' for sure I'd bring Socrates over, I left.

So, now I met Chrys. Dammies! Ah don't know if that's good er bad.

37

Taking Sides

Frederick, the writin' fella, turned out t' be OK. At the first words outta his mouth Ah didn't much care fer 'im, on account of he said, "I'm not going to write letters for you, Mudge, but . . ." An' then's I started liken 'im somewhat better. ". . . I'll be glad to help you. . . . You don't try, you'll never learn."

So we wrote together that it was nice t' hear from mah new partner an' that I was plum honored t' welcome uh new family member.

After we done the letter, Frederick says some nice stuff about mah writin', an' I got t' liken him uh whole lot better. We D-cided t' get together over uh brewski, and Ah went home thinkin' how lucky I was t' meet up with MerryMae what got such nice friends. That got me t' thinkin' she wanted me t' bring Socrates over soz I give her uh call on the telephone t' see if that was alright an she says, "Of course, of course! Come on over now."

It musta been uh good day fer makin' new friends on account Socrates hops off mah arm an' struts right up t' Chrys, and rubs his beak up an' down on Chrys. It were downright amazin' t' see Chrys turnin' bright blue an' then yellow-gold, which is the colors of mah parrot. Socrates didn't say no words but kept up a real low gabblin' to Chrys what kinda blinked some faint colors. Was plain t' see thay was gonna be buddies. Me an' MerryMae hadda nice talk an' after uh while, on account of Ah didn't wanna wear out mah welcome, I says, "Guess we gotta git goin." Well, Socrates started squawkin' and that crystal started shinnin' brown, an' MerryMae was fussin' at me t' stay, soz I asks if Socrates could stay while I went home. That seemed t' make everbody happy, an' MerryMae says, "Come on back for supper, and I'll tell you a funny story I just heard about old Mr. Santé." Well, I knew I'd heard the name, but Ah couldn't place it, an' I guess that showed up on mah face.

"You met him at the party, Mudge . . . elderly gentleman, with all the aches and pains? . . . Samson lives just across the street." She pointed through her picture window t' the little brick house, straight across from this one.

"Oh, yeah, hope it ain't uh story 'bout another operation . . . think I had enough home brewed blood an' guts fer awhile."

"No, no, just a little peek into Mr. Santé's intellect."

Rememberin' back, Ah likely couldn't count on seein' much from just uh peek.

———————◆———————

It were uh good supper, especially there warn't no vegetable pie. MerryMae did make uh mighty tasty rhubarb pie that we washed down with pretty strong coffee, which ain't gonna re place Leinenkugel, but which Ah am beginnin' t' really like an' goes with just talkin' real well.

"I promised you a story, Mudge, so here it is. Last winter, we got new rules about how and when we can park on the streets after a snowstorm, so the plows can clear the streets. It's kind of complicated, so the TV news helps folks by trying to explain which sides are OK for parking after each storm. It seems Mr. Santé and Dolly watch the news faithfully, to catch the snow alerts on parking. We had a several day stretch last winter when it snowed every day, and each day the no-parking directive changed. So, according to Mrs. Foyle, who lives right next door to Sam and Dolly, on that first terribly snowy day the city banned parking that night on the odd numbered address side of the street, and Samson dutifully moved his car to the even side. The next night, the public was instructed to park on the odd side and Sam went out in the snow and cold and moved his Chevrolet to the odd side. Two more nights of snow storm and, of course, two more nights Sam braved freezing temps and biting snow to follow the parking prescriptions. By the fifth day of the storm, however, Samson was so disgusted by the routine that he announced to Dolly, 'To heck with um, tonight, I'm just going to leave my car in the garage.' "

Gosh, there might be more than uh empty peek there, after all.

38

Ya Can't See It Leavin'

Time sure has uh way of disappearin', right in front of ya. Ah remembers uh Spring when the Wet got jammed up with uh buncha snags an' stuff an' the water come way up on Main Street, near flooding Mildred Thudmunson's Parisian Shoppe of Beauty an' Wilber's morticianin' parlor, what's in the back room.

The mayor took uh couple sticks of dynamite an' thrun um inta that pile-up of sticks and D-brie cloggin' up the river. Boy, the water run outta town faster than Billy Good Book when the cops was lookin' fer 'im. Like magic, one minute too much water, the next, it were all gone.

Well, Ah had some recent dynamite sticks of mah own, an' time just sorta blowed by me too. An', on top of that, Ah got mah first ever tax statement from Father Hennepin County. They shortened it up some an' calls it plain old Hennepin County now, but everbody knows it were named from Louis Hennepin uh priest type fella from France er Spain what run the Netherlands back when er wherever. Anyhow, the tax bill's uh duzie. Ah went down t' the courthouse t' pay up an they gotta hugh mung-gus statue of uh fairly naked guy layin' out in the middle of their lobby that Ah figured musta took uh whale of uh lotta tax dollars t' have guys carvin' on it.

Come t' find out, that there statue was uh gift from some rich guys, which in mah opinion, showed what uh grudge they musta had against them courthouse folks. Maybe it were uh sorta sly way of sayin' they didn't like their taxes none neither. But I already learnt that down here in Mini Tropolis they spends money on some strange things, except I gotta add-mitt, that statue guy got the best carved foot I ever seen, an' I'll bet Misty would go plum bonkers if she seen it.

When I got home from the courthouse, the back door was standin' open. It's sorta chilly this time of year and uh open door is kinda invitin' froze up pipes, which kin be uh real K-tas-trophy. At first, I thought it were uh robbin' type break-in an' Socrates got stole, on account he was gone, but nothing else looked took. Then it come t' me, maybe the durn birdie went next door t' visit Chrys, which turned out t' be exactly what happened.

I had uh good talk with Socrates when he got home an' he promised t' always make sure he closed the door when he left our house. Well, he done a good job of door closin' and I didn't have no problems till long about the Spring equal-knocks, an' then it was more of uh problem fer MerryMae, except it were mah parrot what done it.

Socrates never fergot his promise t' close our door, but one day he fergot t' close MerryMae's door when visitin' Chrys, and it got colder than uh Siberian well digger's lunch, in her house. Big problem fer her on account of Chrys didn't wanna do their fortune tellin' act and got riled at the least little thing (like not gittin polished t' his satisfaction) and generally was really off his feed. Ms. Hehm said she never seen him so cranky.

"He just hates the cold . . . originally from Jamaica . . . bought him from a dying voodoo doctor, who made me promise to always love him and keep him warm."

Ah tried t' ease her mind on Chrys, an' X-plained how uh cold ball kin make uh feller downright cranky . . . like the time when Ah went ice fishin' up t' Wet Lake an' had t' sit on the ice all day on account of forgettin' mah campstool. Ah hurt so bad Ah warn't fit fer speakin' t' folks till I could walk proper again. "I'll be glad t' talk t' Chrys," I says.

Told Chrys mah story uh durn near freezzin' off important body parts, an' he starts blinking green. MerryMae said that was a very good sign.

39

Papering Over a Disagreement

The other day I seen Mrs. Foyle grabbin' at something on her roof with uh rake, and went over t' see if Ah could help. Turns out her *SteerTrombone* got flang up there instead of on her porch. We got t' talking on how some folks do their job nowadays an' that led t' speakin' 'bout taxes, an' it ended up she's gonna give me her old *SteerTrombones* fer Socrates' cage. Uh convenience of gittin' rid of old papers fer her will be uh savings fer me.

Socrates overheard me canceling mah sub scrip-shun an' we had uh pretty high-spirited talk 'bout it, but he's pretty reasonable, an finally says, "I suppose the lamebrained things people do will be just as entertaining, even a few days late."

Well, I knowed what he meant by that! I'm kinda took back over birdy's interest in people stuff, like he reads on newspaper r tickles of poly tish-uns an' tax stuff er anything. Of course, his very favorite subject is A-V-A-shun. An' he also specially likes t' find uh r tickle showin' how dumb folks kin be; then I gotta listen t' how birds kin be smarter than people.

We had us uh little argument one day, on that subject, an' Ah got plum X-zass-per-A-ted, sayin', "Listen up mah friend, if you're so smart, how come you're inside the cage an' I'm on the outside?" Boy! I thought Ah had got 'im with a real good zinger. He's quiet fer uh spell an' then he says, "You know who the biblical Ezekiel was?"

"Of course I do. What do you know 'bout biblical stuff?"

Thirty years immersed in academia, Mudge. The Bible, take you're pick of versions, Koran, Kama Sutra, Mahabharata, The Epic of Gilgamesh, Secret of the Golden Flower, to name a few. . . ."

"OK, OK, so ya heard of Ezekiel, what about 'im?"

"You're familiar with the wheels-inside-of-wheels business?"

I said, "Yeah, I read about that, so what?"

"Well," says Socrates, "from my point of view, you're living inside of a cage too. Most folks have a boss, that boss's gotta boss, an on an' on it goes, and, theoretically, they're all governed by rules: your cages. Like Ezekiel's wheels, there's cages-inside-of-cages-inside-of-cages. You're just like me but maybe worse off."

"How's that?" I asked.

"Nobody's changing your papers for ya."

40

GREEN IS RED

I don't know why they calls that durn tax bill uh real estate tax. If it were fake, Ah s'pose Ah wouldn't have t' pay nothin' on it. But real er fake, sometimes Ah think that there tax bill is made uh regular Ebon E-zer Screw-jeh outta me. Like gittin' after Socrates fer un E-conomizin' on food.

I should of never give Socrates uh scoldin' fer throwin' his birdseed on the floor, especially I shouldn't uh mentioned wastin' costs money. Well, he pouted till Mrs. Foyle brung over uh cage-paper with a story that made even big bucks seem like birdseed. He chuckled about a story makin' his wastin' look pretty tame, an' me look pretty cheap. He jumps up t' his swing an' starts squawkin', "Mudge is cheap, Mudge is cheap," till I had t' promise him Ahd never mention birdseed on the floor again.

Anyhow, the r tickle, *Schools' sports turf is artificial, but cost concerns are real,* was about how financially strapped schools manage t' find a million or so t' install that there phony football-field grass. Dammies! If we had grass like that up t' New Boonies, the cows woulda all starved, unless they was phony too. Anyhow, the paper made uh special mention of uh particular school that was rankin' near the bottom. Ah don't think they was bein' nasty on account of they means that school was low down on rankin' in terms of revenue money comin' in. But near uh bottom or not, they still blew more than uh half million bucks t' E-quip their football field with fake grass. Boy! That's the kinda fakin' that would make uh football coach real proud!

Their school Activities Director got quotationed as sayin, ". . . It's an absolutely beautiful sight to see that crisp green field. . . ."

Gosh, that fella looks outta his office an' sees green, the taxpayer's green, but I bet most of us real taxpayers look at them fancy fake fields an' see red!

41

THERAPEUTIC ADVICE

"Hey, Mudge . . . Mort."

"Fer gosh sakes, Mr. Voice-Outta-Mah-Past, what brings ya down under the bus with me?" Ah knowed Mort would git around t' callin' me sometime, just didn't know Ahd feel so strong about it. I was shakin'.

"You get a free a swing at me, Mudge, I deserve it. . . . Anyway, I called to see if you wanted to visit your Aunt, together."

"Why would we do that?" Boy, I was still bein' sharp with Mort while part of me wanted to say, Gosh, I been waitin' fer your call, Mort, an' Ahm real glad t' hear yer voice.

"I didn't think she'd tell you, Mudge . . . you know how she never wants to worry us. But, I'm afraid she might be sick."

"Sick? First I heard. What's the matter?"

"Not sure . . . sounds like it might be something . . . bad, lost significant weight. You know, she was really depressed after hearing about Windsong . . . depressed and shocked. That's when she lost the weight, but now . . . she mentioned something about doctoring and tests, which really isn't like her. That's why I want to go up and see her first hand . . . hoped you'd come with me."

"Of course, I'll come." We had sort of uh little stop in the talking. I couldn't think of nothing to say soz I asked, "How's Misty doin?"

"She's happy as a clam. It's me that's getting the brunt of this thing. . . . Tell you all about it when I pick you up. . . . Tuesday morning OK?"

"Sure."

"See you then, Mudge . . . and . . . I truly am sorry about . . ."

"No need fer sorry, Mort, we're family." My gosh, it felt good t' say that.

———————◆———————

Tuesday turned out t' be uh good day fer drivin': bright enough, but kinda overcast. Mort never eats early, an I didn't have breakfast on account of when I took Socrates next door, Ah got t' chinnin' with MerryMae an' just run t' the car when Mort drove up. Fer more than uh hour we didn't say much but no-account stuff like, "Nice day for uh drive," or uh comment on someone else's bad drivin'.

We stopped at Tobies, in Hinckley, an' hadda cup of coffee and one uh Tobies' special cinnamon sweet-rolls an' that kinda broke the ice on really talkin'.

Mort sets his roll down and wipes the frosting off his fingers. He fiddles with his coffee cup and kinda twists it around like he's thinking how t' start uh real conversation. "I suppose I should tell you the latest about Misty. . . ."

"I'm OK with whatever, Mort."

"I owe it to . . . it's kind of complicated . . . not over yet. Let's get back on the road, you drive, and I'll talk."

———————◆———————

Traffic was real light and I remembers Mort's tellin' about Misty, clear as uh bell.

"You recall that I had mentioned I'd engaged a colleague, Dr. Ogar Shaman. . . ."

"Oh, yeah, the psycho oligist guy. . . ."

Mort gimme one of them funny stares folks do sometimes, like they's thinkin' on what t' say next. ". . . Yes . . . t' counsel Misty. He confirmed my amateur appraisal. . . ."

". . . Foot thing . . . ?"

"Yes, podophilia, but unfortunately, Ogar's first treatment strategy really missed the mark."

"He didn't do his treatment on 'er feet?"

"Oh, he tried to target the foot fetish, by teaching her the metric system . . . wanted to completely purge the word foot from her vocabulary, you know replace it with meter. I thought it was a fairly novel approach, but it proved disastrous."

Mort stared outta the window at uh youngun chasin' some cattle in uh pasture, an' scarin' up uh big flock of returning red-winged blackbirds. He didn't seem t' be enjoyin' the budding spring day; Ah could tell he was thinkin' hard on Misty. Figured it might settle 'im uh mite to talk it out, soz I asked, "What got disastered?"

"Complicated, Mudge. There's probably an inherent danger in theraputic aural substitution. . . . Misty transfered her attentions from foot to meter so intensely that she decided that all the men whose feet she had coveted before her treatment, now wanted to meet her. . . ."

"That's some fancy talkin', Mort, but I gits the meet her."

"That's right, from foot to meter to meet – her. But, I've got to give Dr. Shaman credit, he didn't give up . . . wish he had though."

"Why's that, Mort?"

"Because his next idea was to employ aversion therapy."

"Which was . . . ?"

"He lined up a job for her at Ped Max. You know, the big shoe store down on Lake Street?"

"Oh yeah, they the ones got that slogan sayin', "Ped Max shoes kick the crap out of prices!"

"That's it. Anyway, Ogar felt that Misty would see so darn many feet that she'd learn to hate them and, presto, no more foot fetish."

"Sounds like uh good idea."

"Actually not, whole darn thing backfired. Aversion therapy just didn't seem to work. She wanted to move into the store, make her home there! We had to forcibly remove her."

"Gee, Mort, if that version uh there's-uh-pee don't work, what-cha gonna do?"

"Ogar wants to make one more attempt at the metric thing, to-tally expunge the last vestige of the word, foot, from her mouth."

"Well, whatever version of there's-uh-pee they pick, Ah hopes she kin git her foot outta her mouth, soz she kin git back t' singin'. Little lady gotta mighty fine voice."

"Yeah," says, Mort, "a fine voice and a fractious vice."

Dammies! Feetish er not, Ah hopes he don't put the squeeze onner with one of them.

42

THINGS THAT AIN'T THERE IS?

Durn! Fergot Wet County's never got t' black toppin' the roads, an' with the extra dry spring, by the time we got t' New Boonies, we had enough gravel dust in the car t' start our own rock quarry. Mah asthma was stuffin' up mah lungs near as good as drownin', an' it were uh nice re leef t' pull intah Aunt Thudalia's driveway.

She were in the back garden workin' away with uh hoe. I could tell she didn't hear us till the car door slammed an' she kinda shuffled on her way over. By the time me an' Mort got out of the car an' stretched out the drivin' kinks, Auntie come up t' us.

"You lookin' out fer mah boy proper, little brother?"

"Thuddy, not a day goes by that I don't weep for the lad." Well, they both had a good chuckle over that.

"You just keep them tears aflowin' for um, Throckmorton, or y'all answer t' me."

She was the only person I ever heard that called mah uncle anythin' but Mort. An', she mighta been bent uh little, but her voice was strong an' positive.

"Still got your saucy wits about ya, Thuddy. From that medical report you alluded to, I half expected to find you drooling and babbling."

"No, I'm the same witless old fool I always been, but here we

117

are, all standing around like witless fools. . . . Come on in, wash up an' have uh bite . . . baked uh angel-food fer ya, Throckmorton."

As we entered the only home I'd ever knowed, until I moved, she took my hand, gave it uh squeeze an' said, "An', of course, Ah think we kin find uh platter of fresh corn fritters somewhere."

Familiar as the old house was, I had uh kinda creepy feelin' . . . something was different. Was I feeling funny on account of Aunt Thudalia might be bad sick? Fer some reason it seemed t' be some brighter than Ah remembered. But, mah mind got inner rupted when Mort asks about Aunties' doctorin'.

Aunt Thudalia stopped the coffee cup on the way t' her lips; she lowered it real slow inta the saucer an' just stares at us uh fer uh few seconds, which seemed like quite uh spell. The old wind-up clock, what come clear from Scotland on uh sailin' ship an' then uh Conestoga, ticked off the seconds loud enough t' git heard down t' the mail box by the road.

"I'm through with doctorin', Throckmorton . . . leastwise that's what Ahm told. Ah would uh worked around t' tell you boys afore ya went today, but now it's brought up, I wanna be laid out by the orchard . . . guess it'll be easy diggin'. . . . Hospital re port was pretty definite. Ain't got much more than uh couple months . . . cancer . . . what's got four stages to it . . . guess Ahm about stage six." She smiled. Zingo, Aunt Thudalia's long-haired cat, uh companion of twenty years, just blinked and went back to sleep on her special pillow.

Ah was plum numb. Mah whole body an' mah mind felt like the time we was re parin' Melvin Wigglesword's corncrib an' I clobbered mah thumb instead of uh nail. There wasn't no feeling fer uh few moments, an' then I felt like bein' ripped apart by fire! Mort turned white as uh summer cloud, let out all his breath and sort of faded back onta the sofa.

Suddenly it come t' me. No wonder it was brighter than I'd ever seen it. There warn't uh single one uh them hundred er so Dieffenbachia plants in Aunt Thudalia's house! My mouth just said uh senseless thing. I gasped, "They's gone. Them green . . . they're all gone!"

"Everything's gone when you ain't surrounded by love no more. . . ."

"But . . ." Mah words just stopped. I really wanted t' tell her that she was surrounded by love, lots of it! Yet, Ah knowed she was thinkin' of Johnny, so I just pulled mah chair over an' hugged her fer uh long, long while. Like heart-beats, them ticks of the clock was countin' off Aunt Thudalia's life.

———————◆———————

I wanted t' stay with mah aunt but she said, "No, you go home, Mudge Dear. I can take care of myself just fine, and besides, you've got a parrot to look after. . . ." She lowered her voice and says, "Keep tabs on Throckmorton, I think he might need a hug now and then." I tried to picture mahself huggin' Mort, but ah guess stranger things has happened.

We stood on the back porch sayin' goodbyes. "Aunt Thudalia . . . Ah . . . uh . . . Zingo, I know how much you loves her. . . ."

A little spring breeze sorta played with uh bit of her hair, which had been pure white ever since I could remember. *Ya can't . . . please don't leave me. . . .*

I forgot what I had just said until she said, "Bless your caring heart, boy. . . . Zingo's took care of. Mable Crabtree . . . down towards town?"

"OK . . . if you need anything . . ."

"I can count on you, Mudge, I know that. Goodbye, dear." She gimme uh kiss on the cheek an' whispers, "You and Johnny was the best things in . . . Mudge . . . now go."

———————◆———————

Apples was ripenin' up on the half-dozen trees Aunt Thudalia

119

called her "orchard," an Ah s'pose the other folks what A-tended the burial service thought I was plum crazy. Of course, Ah didn't care what they thought, but I knowed that hugh mung-gus Johnny Dieffenbachia belonged t' sleep with Aunt Thudalia."

43

Uh Little Bit Empty

The little dish of peat moss that holds a small length of Dieffenbachia stem, which I saved from the Johnny plant, makes the room seem empty. An' speakin' of that, I wish Ah could find somethin' t' put in the empty space I got inside, since Aunt Thudalia's passin'. It's funny, just knowin' she was in New Boonies, I didn't think none on how sad I'd be knowin' she warn't there.

I hopes I done that rooting thing right. Ah had watched Aunt Thudalia do uh Dieffenbachia propagatin' thing uh hundred times, but Ah never really seen it t' do it, so, Ah warn't dead sure I done it right. I was pretty careful about not gittin' the juice ontah mah hands on account of, as uh kid, I picked up some of them little stem sections she had fixed, an' got uh rash that burned like forty hornet stings. An' Socrates warn't no help neither on account of he was sorta funnin' me on it.

"Reforestration project? Had hopes you'd abandoned our private wilderness area when you hauled out that green monstrosity."

"Ah never knowed you didn't like it."

For once, he got serious, "Sorry, Mudge. Probably reminded me of the home I never had."

"Home?"

"Yes. I can't say for sure, but from what old Lehrenfalsch said, my mother probably came from Brazil . . . sold to a pet store in St. Paul.

Of course, he never spoke directly to me about it. Can you beat that, Mudge? Thirty years, and he never said a word directly to me . . . just kept me tethered to that damn perch . . . treated me like a feathered decoration. . . . The rest, as your irritating uncle says, 'is history.' "

"Ahd miss ya, Socrates, but if ya wanted t' go home, I'll take ya."

" 'Home I never had.' Had, past tense. Tense, a concept foreign to you."

"I git tense ever once'n uh while. . . ."

"Never mind! Never mind, my home is here, with you, Mudge."

Boy, Ah can't X-plain it, but when Ah heard Socrates say that, our livin' room didn't seem quite so empty.

———————◆———————

I took Socrates next door t' visit Chrys, an' then come home t' call Mort. Boy, was he empty! Misty has took off with uh football player what got size sixteen feet an' Uncle Morton's ang-zi-uh-tin' in the size sixteen range. Seems Misty snuck back t' the Ped Max store an' met this fella in the special sizes D-partment. An', before ya could say Jack Robinson – was unlucky enough t' marry mah grandmaw – Misty and her Big-foot run off together, which I s'pose is easy enough t' run with them size sixteens.

Soz, like Auntie Thudalia warned me on, I guess I gotta hug Mort an' con soul him until he gits hooked up with another ladyfriend.

———————◆———————

Never knowed ladyfriend findin' was so easy. Mort's not empty no more on account of he got took up with Minerva, the Sippin' Singer's alto what looks like uh Goddess an' refers t' Mort as "my little owl."

At first I couldn't tell whooo she was talkin' about. (I make them little jokes all the time.)

44

Givin' Up Tastes Like Surrenderin' or Maybe De Feet

Mort says he got uh conundrum: he wants t' please his new girl-friend, Minerva, who wants t' see him slow down on the Leinenkugels but, on the other hand, he don't wanna cut down on brewski im-bye-been. Ah kin see trouble comin' on account of she's beatin' on Mort's numb drum an' he don't like the sound of that. Ah don't give this relation ship much chance fer smooth sailin'.

———————◆———————

Last Thursday evening was plum uncomfortable. Me an' Mort was chuggin' a few brewskies an', on her break, Minerva come over t' our booth. She was complainin' that the new soprano what replaced Misty "couldn't carry a tune in a suitcase."

"You think Misty will ever rejoin the quartet?" asks Mort.

I caught uh kinda wishful tone in his voice an' Minerva musta picked up on it too.

"Oh, you'd just love that, wouldn't you?" snapped Minerva. She picked up Mort's Leinenkugel can and poured it over his head. There was uh relation ship got scuttled right before mah eyes!

Had t' go intah the bedroom an' close the door on account of Socrates set up such uh racket. Durn! It's like he kin smell Mort on the phone. Anyway, Uncle Morton was so excited when he called Ah thought maybe he'd launch plum t' the moon!

"She's back! She's back! Everything's going to be OK, Mudge . . . now she's back."

"Takin' uh wild guess . . . Misty come home?"

"Yes, yes, dear boy, she's home and I dare to hope she's OK."

"Why don'tcha meet me at the Kaffe Kopp . . . ya kin tell me all about it. Right now Socrates ull wake the dead, if I don't git you off the phone . . . ten tomorrow mornin'?"

"Stupidest thing I ever did, getting you that darned feathered tyrant!"

"Mort . . . don't!"

"OK, OK . . . ten tomorrow morning."

He hung up without sayin' goodbye. Guess he wasn't so happy he could overlook me concernin' fer Socrates.

Ah guess, if Mama Nature gives ya enough time, most bad stuff kin git ironed out. Leastways, that's how it appeared t' be fer Mort. Misty come back to 'im, sayin' how sorry she was fer takin' up with Mr. Size-Sixteen. Seems Bigfoot Boyfriend was also big on wine, which led to a real big case of gout. His size-sixteen Misty-magnets hadda be all bandaged up, an' that's when Misty had t' deal with 'im as a person instead of a pair of big seducin' objects. Guess she realized right away he warn't the fella fer her, an' she come back t' Mort. Intah the bargin, she had lost her fix say-shun on feet.

At the moment, Mort don't need no hugs from me. Misty ain't got no foot ish, an' is back t' singin' with the Sippers. Socrates got uh friend next door, an' I got . . . friends what is happy.

45

KEEPING AN EYE OUT

Mama Nature didn't fergit me after all! It weren't long after Misty come back that MerryMae called, that's the fortune tellin' lady what lives next door, an' asked me an' Socrates t' come over fer uh "mushroom bracer," uh con-cock-shun what she gathers in the woods an' claims is good fer what ails ya. An' if tastin' bad builds better bodies, that stuff beats vegetable pie fer makin' Sampsons outta sissies.

"I'd like your help, Mudge," says MerryMae, "Chrys and I are going to Reykjavik."

"Gee, Ahm sorry, MerryMay, what kin Ah do t' help stop the wreckin'?"

"Not wrecked . . . it's a gig . . . in Reykjavik . . . Reykjavik, Iceland, a big deal for us. And you can help by keeping an eye on our house . . . while we're gone . . . week or so."

"Ya had me worried fer uh minute there, an' no problem, I'll keep an eye on the place here like it were glued smack ontah it."

MerryMae giggles an' says, "Glue OK. No paint this time!"

Well, sometimes folks says stuff what Ah don't catch ontah their meanin' real fast, but I was plum in the dark on what she meant. "How's that . . . no paint?"

Still kinda chucklin' she says, "It's an inside story . . . you know, private joke . . . until now."

You remember the skinny little fellow at the picnic?"

"The feller ate enough hamburgers t' make yer butcher rich?"

"That's the one . . . Pencil Fliddy, the accountant from up the block. Probably shouldn't have invited . . ."

Wow! The room lit up with uh hugh mung-gus flash of purplish light. Socrates, what was sittin' by Chrys, flaps over an' hangs onta the arm of mah chair. Chrys sorta goes from purple t' brown, t' purple uh few times an' settles down t' uh soft blue.

"Oh, don't mind Chrys," says MerryMae, "he gits a little belligerent whenever I mention Pencil. . . . You're so protective, aren't you, sweetheart?" She reaches over t' Chrys and sorta rubs his . . . his . . . gosh durn, don't know what t' say, guess she just rubs 'im.

"Don't know if you noticed, Mudge, but Pencil showed up with dark glasses, a real no-no for him around here."

"Why's that?"

"That's the story. . . . About a year before you moved in, during a warm spell, I was painting the upstairs window frames. . . . Was hotter than a cyclone of chili peppers that day so I dressed real light . . . just an old muumuu. From the top of the ladder, I spotted Pencil, probably walking to the bus stop. He saw me up there and came over t' chat, excepting he stood right below where I was painting. He had on dark glasses and I asked him what he was staring at. . . . Smart-alec says, 'The Heavens.' That done it! So I says, 'Take off them dark glasses and you'll get a better look.' He darn near busted his arm shedding his shades. . . ."

MerryMae give uh devilish little chuckle an' Chrys lit up the room with a couple of yellow pulses, so bright it made Socrates fluff his feathers each time.

". . . That's when I yelled 'Oops!' and doused his 'heavens' up-the-muumuu-staring with my entire bucket of Dutch Boy Midnight-Maroon. . . . Bet the sneaky, peakin' little voyeur was picking red flakes outta his eyes for a month."

"Gee, Ahm surprised he come t' yer picnic."

"Poor little chump thinks it was an accident . . . later, even asked me if he could 'court' me. I bit my tongue to keep from telling the shifty little pervert that the only court we'd ever see together would have a judge and jury. But that ain't the way folks oughta live with each other. . . . I resolved to forget my anger and try to act neighborly, which is why I invited him to our little barbeque."

"Ya kin count on me t' keep mah eye glued t' yer house. Ahm pretty good at lookin' where Ahm s'posed to."

MerryMae gimme uh smack on the arm an' says, "That's because you're an all around good looking guy, Mudge.

46

WHO'S WATCHING WHOM?

MerryMae brung me uh sweater from her N-gage-mint in Icey Land . . . said it were uh gift fer watchin' out fer her house. "I really appreciate your vigilance, Mudge."

I didn't need nothin' fer just watchin', but said, "Thanks," just the same. Sweater had uh big red cross on it, so I figured it was t' wear when ya was savin' folks from fires an' earthquakes an' such, but MerryMae, said it were Icey Land's flag. Well, what with all them volcanoes an' such goin' on there, I kin see why they gotta flag what's the red cross.

"Folks git hurt uh lot while you wuz there?"

"For goodness sakes, Mudge, Reykjavik was quite lovely . . . something like Minnesota, but with volcanoes and hot springs, they even heat homes with their hot springs, day and night"

I tried real hard t' imagine what it would be like t' try an' go t' sleep on springs was that hot, but I s'pose ya kin git used t' most anything. An' fer bein' like Minni Sootah, nothin' gits that cold.

◆

Boy, life kin happen t' ya so fast it's hard t' keep track on it. First, uh savin' sweater, an' then, the very next day, I git in-vited t' Mort an' Misty's weddin', right through the little slot in mah front door. The in-vitation were uh fancy picture of uh hole in some big rock with uh angry lookin' face carved over the door. I recognized Mort's writin' what said, "Misty and I are getting married. Wish you were here!" But, durn! The in-vite was from some place called Bali, an' though me an' Socrates spent more than uh couple of hours lookin' at every little town an' county, the Minni Sootah road map was messed up, an' didn't have it printed nowheres on it. I guess if Mort had uh wanted me there real bad, he'd uh give directions.

But, now Ahm kinda glad I didn't go nowheres, on account of me an' Socrates put that map down when the doorbell ringed. It were Mrs. Foyle with uh bunch of old newspapers. We set uh spell an' talked neighbor-talk an' Mrs. Foyle says, "Next winter, I'm going to visit my sister in Florida. . . . MerryMae says you watched her house while she was away. Could you keep an eye on mine?"

"Be glad to, Mrs. Foyle, mah eye's all practiced up fer watchin'."

Well, it warn't no big step from there to answerin' uh ad in the paper t' uh place what wanted uh X-perienced night watchman fer their warehouse. They gimme uh dark blue uni-form, uh fancy clock I gotta check in on every so often, an uh badge sayin', "Official Security: Amalgamated Associates." I go t' work an' punch in at 11:30 pm an' punch out at 8:00 am, which gives me time before work fer uh few Leinenkugels to keep me company fer the evening.

When Mort got back from his moonin' trip with his honey, he gimme uh call. "Have good news for you, Mudge, Misty managed to convince Johnson that the little incident with your bare foot was all a mistake. . . . They're lifting your *persona non grata*."

"Don't recall dropppin' anything like that, Mort."

"Town Tavern says you can come back . . . no hard feelings. . . . Think their insurance claim got OKed."

"Insurance claim . . . ?"

"Holes in the walls, the roof . . . firemen . . . and the crowd damage."

"Well, I'll be durned. Ain't that just like uh in surance company . . . watchin' out fer me."

47

BORING GOING FULL BORE!

Last Saturday mornin' Ah took Socrates next door t' visit his buddy Chrys, an' MerryMae says t' sit uh spell an' have uh cup of coffee. Didn't take overlong t' say yes, on account Ah ain't had much company lately.

While we was solvin' big world problems an' predicting how bad the poly ticians was gonna mess us up, it re minded me of Mr. Foreman's prediction that mah watchin' job kin git awful boring.

I kinda spilled the beans about how lonely an' borin' mah watchin' job really was, just starin' into uh deserted warehouse the size of uh football field.

"Matter of fact," Ah says t' MerryMae, "on account of a watchin' fella might not catch the sounds of some burglar bustin' in, er uh fire startin' up, we can't have no TV while doin' our watchin' down t' Amalgamated Associates. . . . Sometimes I wanna run outta the place, find somebody willin' t' listen, an' talk till mah throat goes dry."

"Will they let you read?"

"Yeah, but they frown on uh newspaper on account of the big crinkling sounds it makes.

Ya'd be surprised how uh little noise kin behave in there. Ya drop uh pencil, an' it's just uh little click, but ya rattle uh newspaper, an' think uh truck's comin' through the wall."

"How about a book?"

"Ah ain't thought uh . . ."

"Oh, I know, Mudge, . . ." MerryMae interrupts me, ". . . would be a sure cure for boredom!"

"How?"

"You know those little stories you tell . . . about New Boonies . . . your sort of . . . of . . . unusual family, that moved out here from . . . wherever it was . . . Tennessee or Geor . . ."

Was my turn t' interrupt. "Kentucky, they was mountain folk."

"Well, whatever they were, you make them sound really interesting, Mudge, why don't you write about them?"

"Aw, Ah cain't really write none . . . tried to when Ah was uh sprout but . . ."

"Got it! Call Frederick. Guy that did the article on Chrys and me. He might be a big help . . . like . . . that's how I got the gig in Reykjavik, someone saw his magazine story on us, called him and he steered them to me."

"Well, Ah . . . uh . . ."

"I'll set the whole thing up . . . invite him to supper. Of course you'll be here. We can pitch him on it then. You OK with next Saturday . . . assuming the writer is?"

"Yeah . . . I guess." They was all more optimistic about the writin' scheme than I was. MerryMae was already plannin' uh supper menu, Chrys run through uh rainbow of colors, and when we got home, Socrates says, "You'll make a fortune writing about your nutcase Uncle, he's living fiction."

Dammies! Ah don't know what that means, but I kinda like the sound of "fortune"; that ain't boring at all.

48

OF FLUS AND SLIPS AND WEDDING CRACKS OF CABBAGE-HEADS AND STINGS

Writin' turned out t' be uh whole lot uh work, which never were exactly mah strong suit, an' when Ah let it, sorta inter fears with mah con-sump-shun of Leinenkugels. So, gonna finish up the story Ahm workin' on, mostly just fer Frederick, on account he's been uh crack-erjack help an' Ah don't want him t' think I don't appreciate that he's tryin' t' help me. But when this here O-pus is dun, Ahm gonna chuck the whole writin' idea. Besides, right now, Ahm lookin' forward t' Mort an' Misty's wedding celebration which they's throwin' down t' the Town Tavern. Boy, am Ah ever lucky that Johnson, he's their manager, lifted up that personal numb grotto thing soz I kin A-tend.

Mort said I gotta give a toaster to um at the party on account Ahm sorta uh "in absentia" best man. Think Socrates is right-on about "nutcase." Sure don't know how Ah kin give him uh toaster if Ahm ab-sent. So, Ah'll just ignore his fancy in-structions, fergit the toaster, an' give 'im the blender I already bought, an' go to the party just like Ah wasn't s'posed t' be absent.

Ah got t' the weddin' affair early, but Mort an' Misty had already gotten there about uh dozen er so Leinenkugels earlier. So, after huggin' Misty an' shakin' Uncle Morton's hand, Ah had some serious catchin' up t' do.

Johnson had set up uh big, long table with uh pretty buncha flowers in uh fancy vase next t' uh cardboard "reserved" sign, what looked like it had done its fair share of partyin'. Misty joined The Sippin' Singers what sung uh jazzy version of *Auld Lang Syne* an' they was all cryin', except Minerva. Then, they joined us at the "reserved" table, along with their friends an' some of Mort's friends from the University, which was mostly his marchin' buddies, an' everbody was gabbin' an' laughin' until somebody got somethin' down their Sunday throat an' got uh coughin' jag.

The general conversation quieted uh little, an' then the lady next t' the coughin' fella claps 'im on the back so hard he says, "Ow!" That stopped all the talking, an' while it was uh moment of hush, Minerva says, real sarcastic like, "I sure hope you two didn't bring back bird flu from China!"

Mort whispers, "Boy, that stings."

An' then, everybody commenced t' talking, an' O-pin-yun-in', an' clamorin', till one of Mort's buddies raps his spoon onta uh glass an sorta yells, "Hey, folks, listen up! Even China doesn't seem to have a problem now . . . no reported cases here."

Uh lady at the far end of the table says, "I'm not sure that's right . . . just yesterday there was an article in the paper about a Chinese bus driver dying from bird flu."

Wow! Talk about talkin'. It were a talking' del-U-jeh, until Mort bangs on uh glass with his spoon. "Listen . . . listen. . . ."

Nobody did.

"Listen . . . please!"

I thought his rappin' spoon wuz gonna bust his glass, but it did the trick, gittin' most folks t' pay attention. "Listen, I was there. . . . Wasn't at all like the paper described it. . . . Was a bus driver all right . . .

and he died." Boy-oh-boy, that turned on the noise again. It took some mighty good spoonin' t' quiet folks back down. "We were coming back from a trek to the Great Wall, saw the whole incident because we were in a taxi, just behind the bus. You know how newspapers get a few facts and fill in detail with their imagination? Well I was there and saw the poor fellow expire."

"How do we know you're not contagious . . . ?" asked uh fellow I didn't even know. ". . . *Trombone* article said he was a victim of bird flu."

"And he was," answered Mort, "only not what you think. I suppose there was a mix-up when the story was translated. Anyway, the man didn't die from a disease. Flock uh ducks flew into the windshield of his bus, causing him to veer off the road, right into a phone pole – killed him almost instantly – perfect case of dying from the bird flew."

Everybody was plum relieved they had dodged the flu-bullet, an' was gonna live t' enjoy next mornin's hangover, an' went back to im-bye-been free brewskis an' chompin' down Polish sausage. Minerva looked kinda unhappy, I s'pose on account of she couldn't make more trouble fer the newlyweds.

Speakin' of which, Ah never knowed they was in China. "You guys went t' China?"

"We did, indeed, dear boy."

"But China ain't even in Minni Soota!"

"As usual, you are one hundred percent correct, Mudge."

"Whyja go there?"

"Too complicated for your little brain to grasp."

"You callin' me stupid?"

"That was thoughtless of me, Mudge. I apologize, too many Leinenkugels . . . but . . . *in vino veritas*."

"Can'tcha apologize soz Ah kin understand it?"

"Alright . . . means that when we get blasted, we sometimes tell the truth. . . ." Uncle Morton sighs an' hold up his hands. "I'll try again," he says. "*In vino veritas*, it's the Leinenkugel talking."

"I don't know nothin' about vinyl variables, but I ain't dumb enough, er wasted enough, t' swallow no story about talkin' Leinenku-gels."

"OK, I'll translate the Latin for you: in brewski truthski."

"Ah get that . . . Ah guess. . . . An' maybe Ah ain't the fastest brain in the west, Mort, but that don't mean Ah ain't interested in yur China thing."

"Alright, Mudge. I wanted to go for both historical and philo-sophical reasons . . . and besides, it was right on our way to Bali."

"I git it. You was histerical, an' . . ."

"Actually, Mudge, I've always had an itch to see the Great Wall of China . . . exacerbated somewhat by my last little incarceration – remember the trifling disagreement with the law in North Dakota? . . . last time I campaigned for birds, against corporate insensitivity – cramped into that tiny cell I kept repeating, to myself mind you, lines from Frost's *Mending Wall*: 'Something there is that doesn't love a wall, That wants it down.' . . . It was the opportunity of a lifetime. We stopped over in Hong Kong, on the way to Bali . . . so, we just took a junket to the Wall.

"Lemme git this straight, Mort. Ya stopped to see King Kong an' took some junk t' Bali, which Ah tried t' look up but don't seem t' be nowheres around here."

"That's right, Mudge. Bali's right where it's always been, Indo-nesia."

"In dough knees ya . . . thought that was somethin' folks got when they couldn't remember nothin'."

"That's am ne . . . never mind, my boy. Bottom line is, we're glad to be back, and happy to see you."

Boy, I ain't never gonna forgit that.

49

WISE-CRACKS IN A RELATIONSHIP

Uncle Morton says he's frustrated on account of now he's married up. He told me he had uh real fine offer from some university in California t' be the head of their D-part-mint studyin' on "Realizing Metaphysical Post-materializations," says it's the latest thing there. "It's cutting edge, Mudge, but Misty doesn't want to leave The Singers." Actually, I was real glad Mort ain't gonna leave on account I'd miss 'im quite uh bunch. Even though nowadays about the only time I see 'im is on Thursday evenings, down t' the Town Tavern.

"I understand they got uh traffic mess out there, Mort, ya might not like the place, anyhow."

"Why?"

"Seen it on TV. Seems there's so many cars, an' so many folks marchin' fer stuff, they took their traffic an' their grids an' locked um up.... Know how you like marchin' an' all, an' of course, ya mench-und at the weddin' party how ya ain't partial t' walls."

"The TV report say anything about gridlock?"

"Sure did! You musta seen it too."

"No, but now I know where you're coming from."

"Oh, Mort. Ya always knowed where I come from. We both come from New Boonies."

"And speaking of New Boonies, dear boy, I understand you're

writing stories of our New Boonies' ancestors."

"Howja knowed that?"

"A little bird told me."

"Aw, come on, Mort, Ahm too old t' believe in little birdies an' Socrates is too big t' be little . . . an' besides, you two don't never talk, just screech an' shout. So tell me, howja know?"

"I met your nice neighbor."

"Ah got lots of neighbors, Mort."

"This one had a kiosk at the Marvel Mall. She was making appointments to foretell people's future."

"MerryMae! Ya musta met mah fortune tellin' neighbor, MerryMae."

"She spoke very highly of you, Mudge. I'd say she really likes you. . . ."

"Nice of her t' say so. . . ." Ah waved Sally over an ordered a couple more Leinenkugels. ". . . What was you doin' at the Marvel?"

"Marching, with the team . . . so proud of them, the whole team turned out!"

"What was ya marchin' fer, this time?"

"Reducing crowds in public spaces. . . . We've got a real problem there. . . ."

Ah didn't say nothing about them marchin' felllas adding t' the crowd at Marvel Mall.

". . . But tell me about your writing. I thought your documentary skills evanesced after you put down your name . . . and you're going to write about our relatives?"

"Givin' it uh try." Ah didn't like his big words . . . didn't knowed what they meant, but I kin smell sarcasm when Ah hears it. Maybe he should go t' California.

50

Uh Right Smart Way t' Write

Since Mort got hisself matro moneyed up, he seems t' of lost uh little gung-ho fer Leinenkugelin' on Thursday evenings. Says he sees enough of Misty soz Sippin' Singer nights ain't so special, an' maybe he's includin' me. He don't say nothin' about it no more, but Ah think he's plum disappointed he didn't take that perfessor's job in California. I hope I ain't paranoin', but me an' Mort just never got real comfortable with each other after Misty's foot ish thing. Guess Ahm real lucky t' have uh friend like Socrates an' uh new thing t' do, which is writin'. Changed mah mind again on that. Fer uh while, wuz gonna give writin' up on account it were more work than I thought an' I had got stuck trying t' figure out the right way t' tell uh story.

Well, Frederick, he's the writin' feller, come t' the rescue on that. He said, "When you think you're stuck, Mudge, try imagining that you and I are having a cup of coffee, and you're telling me about whatever. Just write it down that way."

"Where we havin' our coffee?"

"Doesn't make much difference, anyplace where you're relaxed."

"Would that work the same if Ah imagined we wuz havin' uh couple of Leinenkugels?"

"Imagination is a writer's best tool, Mudge. Try it both ways . . . see what works."

Boy! That Frederick is uh smart guy, but Ah think he kinda messed up on the tool thing. Of course, not wantin' t' hurt his feelings none, Ah didn't mention uh good sharp pencil is likely the best writin' tool, but Ah says, "Ahm gonna imagine tellin' ya uh real favorite family story, 'bout one of Wet County's famous first business guys . . . he were uh shirt-tail relative of some sort. Matter of fact, there's still uh few Mathewses liven' around New Boonies, but this here story took place way back when."

51

WAY BACK WHEN

Way back when, some of mah ancest-tree-all family heard stories of how great, great Grandpa Thudmunson found uh place what didn't have no sheriff er nobody t' inter fear with folk's private doin's. Them what was fed up with all them rules an' laws of civil-lie-zation, what they had in hill-an'-holler Kentucky, commenced comin' t' New Boonies, where they figured thar warn't no long-armed law fellers behind every tree. Uh place, where uh body could shoot uh troublemaker intah per-dish-un an' that was that – on account ya can't git back from there t' dish out no more trouble. Of course, they was wrong on account of them stories got X-zagerated, but that didn't stop folks from believin' in uh "promised-type land" an' it didn't stop some of um from comin'.

Accordin' t' Aunt Thudalia, one of them early settler folks comin' from Kentucky t' New Boonies become mah relative after he got here, on account of marryin' up with Effie Wigglesword. He were uh preachin' fella name of LukeSimon Mathews, an' left apple-lay-she-uh t' git uh fresh start. He needed uh new beginnin' on account of when he was sermonizin', he was partial t' holdin' up rattlin' snakes as an X-pression of confidence that higher powers would protect him. Unfortunately, there was uh incident where he held one of his lethal helpers too close t' uh wheel-chair-bound parishioner who had paid in advance on uh two-fer-one special; LukeSimon claimed he could make the man walk again an save his soul, all in one sitting, or standing, whichever.

There transpired somewhat of uh discombobulation when LukeSimon held the twisting viper out to the crippled feller, but due t' a soreness problem in his back, accidentally dropped it, which tangled the snake inta uh wheel on the chair. The serpent, which they say was ordinarily pretty tame, got pinched, which un-tamed it in a hurry. It started bitin' everythin' in sight an' bit the Billy-be-gosh-durned outta the poor wheelchair fella, expirin' him on the spot.

Well, the relatives of the un-mortalized guy wanted the pre-payment back, claimin' LukeSimon didn't earn his money on account of the D-ceased never got up an' walked, an 'further, thar warn't enough time fer his soul t' git really saved, but – an' Ahm just guessin' on this here –they was likely uh bit uneasy about rilin' some big fella way up yonder, so they was willing t' compro-mise uh few dollars on the soul-savin' point.

LukeSimon countered by assertin' that he had uh strict no-refund policy, spelled out by uh sign in big letters at the front of the meetin' room, just under the "Have Faith in Believing" sign. An' then his lawyer laid out uh big legal R-gument, sayin', "Rampant recidivism among savees requires further ecclesiastical labors, usually at no fur-ther remuneration, which justifies a 'no-refund policy.' "

I guess the judge was un-impressed. They say he said, "Dag-nab it, if ya want the court t' listen, speak English."

There followed uh buncha pros an uh buncha cons, but E-ven-tually, LukeSimon's fate seemed t' kinda hang on his character witness, Chester Winelove. Chester was uh deacon in LukeSimon's preachin' en-terprise an' a partner in their moonshine business, but he didn't show up, sendin' his wife with a note sayin' he couldn't come to court on ac-count of he had t' git uh barrel of ripe mash t' distillin' soz the custom-ers wouldn't suffer no throat parchin', but he'd be by the next day.

Well, accordin' t' family tellin', the judge got pretty snappish an' ordered up uh new trial fer moon shining without no permit, which wuz never permitted no how anyways, an' he set bail so high, it mostly

146

cured preacher LukeSimon's sore-back problem, on account of it durn near emptied the stash under his mattress.

That stirred up the local sheriff what was peeved on account of LukeSimon had been holdin' out on his sty-pend. An' it brought on the County Constable on account nobody had told him about Luke-Simon an' Chester's operation an' the possibilities of uh courtesy-type payoff. The Federal Revenuers got involved becaue LukeSimon had fer-got t' contribute t' Congressman Larson's last campaign, an' everybody knowed he always got even with cheap contributin' con-stit-U-ants by sickin' the Feds onto um, 'specially if they was runnin' stills.

The upshot of all the legalin' was that LukeSimon skedaddled off t' New Boonies; I s'pose he figured it would be a fresh supply of folks thirstin' fer savin' and thirsts needin' quenchin'.

He's re-phew-ted, by local historians, t' have told folks, "I just had faith that New Boonies would have its share of rattlesnakes an' im-bye-bers . . . an' of course, Ah liked the name."

Well, Wet County had enough im-bye-bers t' make uh moon-shiner walk on water in happiness, an', though LukeSimon's faith could make lame folks walk, till the crowd left, it warn't quite up t' bringin' rattlesnakes wrigglin' inta Wet County. Turned out that there warn't much of uh rattlesnake supply around New Boonies but Providence, or maybe the big guy up yonder, stepped right in an' provided.

Whilst visitin' Duluth t' spy on his competition, uh re-vivalist tent show that had uh trumpet player what was six an' uh half foot tall, an' uh banjo plucker, LukeSimon took in uh travelin' circus. He was so impressed by the snake charmer's cobra, he decided t' give the poor beast uh better life than circusin', an' when nobody was lookin', plopped the snake inta the rattlesnake bag he always carried.

The cobra proved t' be uh bigger curiosity than the freaky-tall trumpet player an' pretty soon the tent folks folded it up an' went t' tend flocks in other pastures. For LukeSimon, competition was gone and life was good. An' fer uh time, Providence, or maybe the big guy up yonder, also saw to it that none of the folks, what dropped quarters intah the collection plate that LukeSimon passed around, got bit t' death. But, there come uh time when The Infinite musta took uh pass on protectin' duty an', wouldcha know it, that was the very moment the cobra turned on LukeSimon an' sunk its fangs deep into its keeper's arm.

Some have speculated that LukeSimon was not a man off blood and bone, but rather, moonshine and machination. Family lore has it that, after withdrawing it's fangs, the serpent thrashed about for less time than required to sing uh couple verses of the National Anthem, an' then went die-wreckt-lee t' the big ophidiarium in the sky.

If LukeSimon had just had sense enough to let his snake's death ride, his survival was of such a novelty that it probably would have drawn the curious and the righteous to his sermons, filling the collection plate with enough quarters to insure a dignified retirement. He could have given up moonshining and entered the ranks of honest citizens. But greed for much seems to extend to greed for a little; it was LukeSimon's undoing. He should never have demanded that the County pay uh bounty on the expired cobra on account of the County never paid uh bounty on nothing. Well, LukeSimon left the dead cobra in uh cardboard box in the County office which kept remindin' the clerks uh little more every day it stayed there, that the stale mate needed resolvin'. Finally, when just openin' the windows didn't really help no more, an' county official dumb just couldn't tolerate the smell no longer, they figured the preacher would come take his snake if they started an in-vest-T-gation inta his moonshine operation, which everbody in the countryside knowed of, but not much about.

Well, LukeSimon was too crafty fer um. They couldn't find uh jot uh ev-E-dense t' catch 'im on moonshinin', but he warn't so careful with his preachin' business. Once uh invest-T-gay-shun got goin', uh lotta folks come forward with complaints on how they had t' buy back their wooden leg er crutches an' stuff. One feller paid uh hundred dollars up front but still had t' mortgage his best heffer t' buy his son's wheelchair back.

LukeSimon didn't have no sympathy fer any of um, sayin', "Can I help that these whiners don't have sufficient faith to walk? Besides, I got papers they signed; it's all legal."

On uh positive note fer LukeSimon, uh lady come forward sayin' LukeSimon's cobra bit her seeing-eye dog t' inta demisement an' though she didn't have no money fer uh new dog, LukeSimon offered her uh ten percent discount on a cane what he had; all that needed doin' on it was t' paint it white.

About then is when Judge Harden Steel got involved. He was quoted as sayin', "It's time we brought this snake charmer to justice . . . before he 'saves' the whole county . . . from sobriety." An' sure enough, it warn't long before LukeSimon was undergoin' uh good courtroom grillin' by the County's – an' maybe the world's – meanest judge.

"Mr. Mathews, I understand a snake in your possession died after biting you in the arm."

"Yes Sir, yer Honor, the critter went belly-up not twenty minutes after savagely attackin' me."

"Why do you suppose the beast expired?"

"Coulda been most anything, fang fatigue disorder . . . old age, maybe?"

"Lets not spar further, Mr. Mathews. You are well known in this County to be a purveyor of alcoholic spirits and . . ."

"That's the second time you've disrespected my collar. I'll thank you t' address me as, 'Reverend,' yer Honor."

"Very well, 'Reverend.' Do you admit the snake may have died from consuming your noxious concoctions?"

"I have no idea to what you refer."

"Oh, come now, everyone in the County is aware of your . . . alter-entrepreneurism. . . . Word is, you make the finest white lightening west of Tennessee."

"Though, of course, you can't prove it . . . your Honor."

"Let's try a different tack, then. . . . Reverend, do you consume alcoholic beverage?"

"I do."

"Admitting guilt to nothing, can you share with the court the degree of your consumption?"

"Certainly, sir. In a word, copiously . . . probably what saved my life."

"And, perhaps, what killed your . . . ah . . . pet."

"My partner in salvation is more accurate."

"Very well, but the court will assume that if your life were saved by the purity of moonshine in your veins, that must have been the very agent causing your . . . 'partner's' demise."

The story is that the gavel banged loud enough to startle folks back in Kentucky.

Judge Harden Steel warn't gonna let no slick-tongued, snake healin' hillbilly flout Minnesota law; he give LukeSimon Mathews two years in the Minnesota Territorial Prison for "failure to register a venomous creature as a dangerous weapon" and "feeding unauthorized toxic material to wildlife without a license."

They let LukeSimon outta the hoosegow early on account of good behavior an' he never again took up with no serpents. Family lore has it that he always used t' say, "Who needs snakes, when folks got thirst's need quenchin'?"

52

BS Don't Always Mean Best Story

Wow! This here writin' stuff is easy. All Ah gotta do is remember how Aunt Thudalia told her stories, like:

Everbody knowed that Nerdon Dagget were the best criminal lawyer in Wet County. Mainly, that were on account of he wuz the only criminal lawyer that wern't caught yet. Some said his lawyerin' warn't near as good as his criminalin' but "if it takes a thief to catch a thief," and you wuz a law-breaker needin' a lawyer – well, you git the picture. Nerdon was always knowed fer his slipperiness, but it was Titus v. Kiddle that slid 'im right inta the spotlight an' made him uh big-time BS lawyer. The case involved two neighbors what was diss-phew-tin over a contract they had made about stud services.

Ya coulda turned one uh them long-distance type pigeons loose, let it fly in any direction till it dropped, an' it woulda likely never flew over uh man what was more tight-fisted than the complainant, Andrew Titus. On the other hand, defendant Fenton Kiddle had earned his reputation for slick dealing the hard way, one dissatisfied customer at a time; by the time his youngest boy graduated outta the fourth grade, nobody in Wet County trusted him. And, when them two fellers clashed in court, it were uh X-zample of uh irresistible force whackin' inta that there immovable object folks tells about.

Oddly, them two guys had quite uh bit in common. They both

raised Black Angus beef cattle fer a livin', and wuz also knowed t' raise an occasional ruction down t' the Grand Saloon in New Boonies. The gossips all said that they wuz both pretty well limbered up when they wrote out a contract stipulatin' uh $300 stud fee, right there on the bar, for Fenton Kiddle's bull to service Tillyfour, Mr. Titus' prize angus heifer. That heifer was knowed all over the county as Not-so-Fast Tilly, on account of she only calved once, courtesy of uh long-armed, syringe-wielding veterinarian; so far, none of her suitors were t' her likin', she'd just stuck up her pretty black muzzle, an' wouldn't have nothin' t' do with um. An' she meant business. A couple of Kiddle's hired hands tried t' hold her for a bull once, and I guess one of um is still usin' uh cane t' git around.

But the bull in question, Black Prince of Galloway, was responsible for a slew of dark descendants and Kiddle was sure his Prince would overcome any dating scruples held by the picky Not-so-Fast Tilly, so sure, that he made an intemperate offer, overheard by near everybody in the Grand.

"If Prince don't cover your durn persnickety cow, you can have 'im."

"We can put that in the contract?" asked the flabbergasted Titus, perhaps not quite as far down in his cups as Kiddle.

And that was how the whole mess ended up in the courtroom of Judge Harden Steel, and earned Nerdon Dagget the note-er-riot-T of a real BS attorney.

◆

Word gets around pretty easy in New Boonies and everybody an' his brother turned up at the Titus farm on the day of the big event. There wuz so many folks sittin' on the fences that Titus had t' clear some of um off t' keep the rails from bustin'. Sheriff Thudmunson was overheard askin' Mr. Titus if he wanted some of the gawkers run off but Titus said, "Gosh no, just in case . . . the more witnesses the better."

The big moment come when Andrew Titus led Tillyfour outta the barn, an' inta the nuptial corral. They say she held her head high, like a grand lady, and stood real patient, some said she just looked bored, while her bridle was took off. She gives her head uh little twisting shake when there come bangin' an' crunchin' sounds from the rocking stock trailer parked at the far end of the corral. The crowd could tell that the Black Prince of Galloway was eager to improve the Kiddle bank account by another three hundred bucks, an' they let out uh whale of uh cheer. Tillyfour shakes her head as though sayin', "I don't like none of these noises," and sashays back toward the barn.

Mr. Titus starts shouting, "Please, please, stop!" He was runnin' around the corral, wavin' his arms an' beggin' fer quiet. After folks got settled down t' just talkin, Mr. Titus give the signal to open up the trailer.

Prince come snortin' down the little ramp and trotted over in back of Tillyfour, all set to do his duty. The ebon heifer turned to face her suitor, an' fer uh moment it looked like she was interested in Prince Charming. And then, for reasons known only to the dark damsel, she tossed her head and trotted back toward the open barn door. The Prince, anxious to save his damsel from spinsterhood, made a clumsy attempt to complete his mission, but like a fairytale, the damsel recalcitrantly morphed to Not-so-Fast Tilly, and butted Black Prince in the side. As she disappeared into the maw of the barn, the rejected wooer docilely allowed himself to be wrangled back into his trailer.

◆

Black Prince of Galloway felt no ignominy. His failed tryst was just another day at the office where the deal fell through. Any shame attached to the unfulfilled transaction, attached to Fenton Kiddle, the butt of taunts and whispering, especially from patrons at the Grand Saloon who had witnessed him returning three hundred dollars to Andrew Titus. Not sufficient recompense, however, as shortly, Fenton

Kiddle found himself in the toils of the law. Titus demanded that, according to their contract, Kiddle pony up – maybe bovine up – his most prize possession: Black Prince of Galloway.

The New Boonies betting crowd wuz forced to give odds, sometimes as high as 4 to 1, in favor of the penny pinching Titus. He was a seasoned litigant (a sorta nice way of sayin' he sued folks at the drop of a hat), had hired a devious lawyer, the simple contract, which had become common knowledge, seemed straight forward in his favor, and, the clincher, Kiddle had elected to represent himself – in Judge Harden Steel's courtroom – probably justification for 10 to 1 odds.

———————◆———————

Judge Steel glared at the newly empaneled jury. "I want you to remember that Justice may be blind, but she's not dumb." It ain't knowed if he ever give uh thought that there warn't even one real peer of Fenton Kiddle in the jury box; everyone from New Boonies who could walk, hobble, or hop had attended the attempted insemination.

The jurors were mostly from Huns Point (one was from Millerton, one from No Where, MN) but a parade of New Boonies witnesses confirmed the incident, one after another, until the Judge said, "Enough . . . enough." The simple fact emerged: Not-so-Fast Tilly had lived up to her sobri-K, the black beauty had spurned the Black Prince.

Titus' lawyer could of, an' sure as grass is green should of, probably let it go right there, but insisted on making a statement.

"Alright, let's hear it . . . but, please, Mr. Dagget, don't make it overlong." They say the Judge leaned back an' closed his eyes. Maybe he was listening or maybe he was imagining hisself fishing in Mercy Cove over to Wet Lake.

"Your Honor, and members of the jury, from fictional lawyers like the wealthy heiress, Portia, to real life defenders of justice such as Bryant or Clarence Darrow or . . ."

Judge Steel's eyes popped open; he sat up as though stuck with a pin. "Yes, yes . . . please conclude your statement, Mr. Dagget. . . . You have inspired the court."

"Oh, ah . . . well, all those lawyers were interested in justice, Your Honor . . . and, ah . . . so am I . . . and, of course, my client."

"Thank you sir. . . . Summations. . . . Mr. Dagget."

Nerdon Dagget straightened his tie and approached the jurors. "Good citizens of Wet County, you have all seen copies of a document that clearly states that should Mr. Fenton Kiddle's bull fail to cover my client's cow, my client, Mr. Andrew Titus, shall assume title and ownership of Fenton Kiddle's bull.

You have listened to the testimony of twelve impartial witnesses, that the bull in question did not perform according to the terms of the agreement . . . the contract. Therefore, I ask you to enforce the terms of the contract and award title to said bull to Mr. Titus. . . . Thank you." Dagget resumed his seat.

Mr. Kiddle's summation would probably not be cited in many law schools as exemplary. "That chiseler shouldn't get my bull. . . . I was drunk." He sat.

The jury strung out their deliberations and ran into the noon hour, probably t' get a free lunch on the County. Following their repast, a speedy verdict was rendered: "We find for the plaintiff."

However, they weren't excused as quickly as they had hoped. Judge Steel decided to render a statement of his own. "I commend the jury for it decision. The court agrees, the contract is clear and unambiguous, and the adduction of the central fact is corroborated by many, no doubt unimpeachable, witnesses." He directly addressed the smiling, new owner of the Black Prince of Galloway.

"Now, Mr. Titus, your attorney has brought up an interesting point, one which the court finds worthy of consideration. . . . I have driven past your farm on many occasions. . . . Tell me Sir, do you still have that colorful sign by your mailbox?"

"Sure do, Your Honor."

"Can you recall the text of your sign?"

"The what?"

"What does the sign say, Mr. Titus?"

"Oh, that's easy. It says, 'Grade A Manure for Sale.'"

"Anything else?"

"Oh, yeah, it says, 'Our manure grows the best silverbeets and pieplants,' but that was painted on as sorta a extra there. . . . The Missus suggested that an' . . .'"

"Thank you Mr. Titus. . . . How is your . . . ah, manure sold, by the pound or . . .'"

Maybe Andy Titus smelled uh sale or somethin', an' he interrupts the Judge. "You can have it any way ya want it, Your Honor. Sells in hundred pound gunny bags or, if ya want a fair amount, I can run a truckload out to ya or if . . .'"

Judge Steel raps his gavel, and Mr. Titus gets the hint t' stop talkin'. "And, what is the cost of . . . say, a one hundred pound bag of . . . of . . .'" His Honor, not usually lost for words, seemed searching for something. "Of your commodity." He paused. "Let's invent our own little shorthand here. . . . Hereafter, for identification purposes, lets just refer to your product as BS. . . . I abbreviate from your reference to Best Silverbeets.

"Now, please give the court your latest price on a one-hundred pound bag of BS."

"Four bucks a bag . . . but for you, Judge, I'd make it three fif . . .'"

The gavel descended with silencing authority.

"Then you do agree, Mr. Titus, that BS has an established commercial value?"

"Oh, yes, Sir . . . it's . . . ah, BS is valuable stuff." They say Andy Titus smiled and puffed out his chest, looking very pleased with himself, for using Judge Steel's "little shorthand."

"One more question, Mr. Titus. Would you agree that your new acquisition, Black Prince of Galloway, is a regular producer of BS?"

"Oh, yeah, Your Honor . . . he's full of it!" Andrew Titus smiled and turned to look at the gallery, which was snickering. The gavel silenced the courtroom, and probably prevented Titus from taking a bow.

"Very well, I have information for you that may influence your future humorous recitals. By your act of accepting Mr. Kiddle's bull, you are simultaneously depriving him of a valuable commodity, namely BS, which he in no way granted to you in the contract that you have insisted on enforcing. By accepting Dark Prince, you are committing larceny, to what extent might only be determined by how long you retain ownership of said BS producer." The judge's glare seemed to burn a hole in Andrew Titus's chest. Some even said they expected to see his shirt front start smokin'. "Mr. Titus, do you know how this court regards those attempting larceny?" Without waiting for an answer, Judge Steel thundered, "I send them to prison and throw the key away!"

His Honor waited patiently for the undercurrent of gabbling to quiet and adopted a conciliatory tone. "Now, off the record, mind you, I would suggest that you and Mr. Dagget work out an arrangement with Mr. Kiddle, one where the court would not be obliged to seek criminal sanctions."

Nerdon Dagget rose and addressed the court. "May we adjourn, Your Honor, for the purpose of reaching a . . . an . . . amicable resolution." Andy Titus tugged at Nerdon's sleeve. "As a matter of fact, Your Honor, my client has just advised me that he wishes to dismiss his claim, if the defendant will so stipulate."

"Why, Mr. Dagget, what a grand idea. I am always pleased when litigants decide to amicably resolve these BS cases."

53

Two Birds with One Stone

Ah cain't really figure out Frederick; he's uh nice guy, but he don't seem t' have no interest in Leinenkugelin' . . . guess we all have little character D-feks. Anyway, we met up at the Kaffe Kopp, where Frederick says we can "fika" while he gimme uh cry-Teek on mah *Way Back When* an' *BS* stories. Boy! He was pretty durn encouragin', even if he did dawdle over his Lingonberry cake, an' made some pretty lame comments on the weather we's been havin'.

Ah am real anxious t' hear what he got t' say on mah story, but he fiddles some more an' wipes off his fingers – what was strange on account of he ate his cake with uh fork! Another of them Pee-culiarities he got. Finally, he gits down t' mah writin'.

"I think you have some definite strengths, Mudge . . . real sense of story, colorful descriptions, some unusual word juxtapositions. . . ."

Gee, Ah hope he don't go Mort on me . . . durn two-bit words.

". . . And I'd say all you have to work on is proper tense, pay attention to point-of-view, watch for the infinitives you split, and try to use a more standard syntax. . . . Remember, forcing nouns into verb form is fairly unorthodox – which you do a lot – and just a few minor clause rearrangements will help this." He patted mah man-U-script, which Ah noticed got uh big wet coffee ring onta it. . . . "Oh, before you finish up a story, check the spelling, that's important. Take care of those things, and you'll be on your way."

"Gee, thanks fer them encouragements."

"And just one more thing, Mudge . . . you know what a run-on sentence is?"

"No."

"Uh, that's OK, for now . . . just don't loose heart, there's lots of different tastes out there, and someone's bound to like your style."

Boy! Them was words Ah liked. Ah am on – mah – way . . . an' somebody's gonna like it!

Think Ah got me another story tryin' t' come out, one what I wuz re minded on by the last story, on account of it's about New Boonies uh fair time back.

———————◆———————

Ya already knows about old, snake-wavin' LukeSimon Mathews an' tough old Judge Steel on account of they were mah last stories. What ya don't knows is that, after LukeSimon got outta the Territorial Prison, he an' Effie Wigglesword married up an' had themselves uh little girl, Mildred, an' though her Daddy wanted her t' take up the preachin' pro fession, he had t' wait fer uh grandchild, t' carry on the family business.

Mildred went inta matra money with her third cousin, Jake Thudmunson, and their firstborn child, Grover, filled all the dreams old LukeSimon had of uh preacher t' take up the reins of the family enterprises – almost. Seems Grover Thudmunson took on preachin' about as serious as uh fella could, but when it come t' tendin' uh still, er even peddlin' moonshine, he didn't want nothin' t' do with it. But, Providence be praised, the thirsty citizens of Wet County didn't do no expirin' from parchment; it were one of them things what works out with Mama Nature, on account of uh big liquor wholesaler in Duluth dropped prices on whisky t' the point it drove all the independent moonshiners in northern Minni Soota right outta businessin' – almost.

The main holdout was Grover's younger brother, Grimly,

whose Granddad, old LukeSimon, happily taught the intra-cussies of home brewing. Well, Mama Nature stuck her big nose inta the family preachin'/moonshinnin' E-kway-shun and sent uh hor-riffic fulmination of lightening, t' strike the liquor warehouse in Duluth, burnin' it an' all its contents t' uh fair amount of sooty smithereens, uh case of White Lightening's big brother, Sky Lightening, righting an injustice.

Grimly was quick t' point out t' his big brother that Providence had opened the door for the families' bibulous enterprise to prosper, once again. It's actually writ down, that Big brother, Grover, thundered, "Though all the hounds of hell guard your evil endeavor to corrupt by illicit spirits, I will oppose every drop of the Devil's brew you conjure!" Well, almost anybody could guess that Grover warn't much of uh drinkin' man.

Them boys didn't git on over-chummy after that, an' gradually, it got t' where they didn't even speak t' each other. However, each one prospered at his own profession, an' they become the most influential men in New Boonies. Them boys worked so hard at what they done, neither of um had never give family er matra money uh thought. They wuz dead D-kated!

Like most things in Nature, give stuff enough time, and even fightin' things sorta reach uh kahm-pro-mize. Was like that with Grover an' Grimly, each one had his territory staked out an' they was happy igg-norin' each other. They was status quoin' it quite nice until Mama Nature used Duluth to provide, for a second time (or uh third time, dependin' on how far back ya go), and plopped down the one thing New Boonies had uh shortage of: uh dee-zirable lady.

"Constance Elizabeth Cromwell can not hide her slender, hourglass form, though dressed fully in black, as proper for a woman in mourning. A petite nose shares space with lively brown eyes, a narrow silver streak runs through a mass of jet curls, like a shaft of morning sunlight piercing a shadowed garden. Her general demeanor is of studied seriousness, just slightly belied by a barely suppressed smile hovering about her ever so slightly too-sensuous mouth." That's how old Grover Thudmunson described Mrs. Cromwell in a letter to a colleague. In fact, the forty-something bachelor was so smitten with the lady, he called unannounced, to welcome her to the fair community of New Boonies.

Grover inquired, very delicately Ah assume, how the lady came to town, an' was informed that Silas Wigglesword, the recently deceased owner of the NB Lumberyard, had discovered some degree of relationship to her family when on a business trip to Duluth, and, "lo and behold," she now owned "an enterprise of considerable substance." Oh my! This was a "two birds with one stone" opportunity, procuring a most desirable mate and "an enterprise of considerable substance" by one effort; what could stand in the way of such golden serendipity?

Practically nothing, except a handsome younger brother who was equally determined to pluck this luscious fruit from the tree of good-fortune.

Presented with suitors of such severe polarity, Mrs. Cromwell evidently followed her instincts, opting for youth and lightening (of the white variety) over sobriety and rectitude. Therefore, it was ere long after the lovely lady from Duluth first dazzled New Boonie's swains, an announcement of engagement in the *Huns Point Herald* foretold the intention of matra money the following spring, between said lady and Wet County's most prominent law-breaker, breaking the heart of Wet County's most prominent righteous man.

The elder brother was determined to derail the impending nuptials, but of course, he couldn't be seen as some cowardly poltroon, removing a section of the marriage bound track. An' then, an idea struck 'im: run uh bigger locomotive smack inta his brother's nup-chew-al train, a killer locomotive that he could surreptitiously switch onto his brother's track, but engineered by others. His killer locomotive would be called: The New Boonies Righteous Shepherd's Lodge.

Grover gathered all the male friends he could muster, to form a public bulwark against vice and iniquity. Committees were formed to address, and hopefully rectify, specific community ills. Thus sprang groups of men dedicated to the problems of horse-beatin', public de-bauchery, iniquitous enabling agents like saloons and moonshiners, and wife-abuse, each a committee chaired by a prominent person. As founder, Reverend Grover was duly consecrated as Exalted Shepherd of the Crook, which nobody didn't seem t' notice the irony of, and as-sumed Chairmanship of the Wife-Abuse Committee; he reasonably explained, "As I am not married, my judgments regarding this Com-mittee's business will be purely impartial."

He saw to it that petty thief, an' minor competitor of his brother, Filcher Lootmann, was appointed Chair of the Iniquity Enabling Com-mittee, suggesting that "Filcher's experience with the law seems ideal to treat with those enabling crime and sottenness." All agreed, Reverend Thudmunson's brilliance was only matched by his piety and devotion to virtue.

There is no record of how Filcher Lootmann discovered the lo-cation of Grimly Thudmunson's frequently moved distillery and stor-age sheds. Some whispered that someone close, like family, B-trayed him. Most, however, credited The New Boonies Righteous Shephards Lodge for doing its committed duty. Besides, public attention was fo-cused on the apprehension of Wet County's no-torious moonshiner, along with seventy-three barrels of whisky what was "smoother than uh baby's bottom."

Grimly pulled thirty-eight months in prison and his brother, Reverend Grover, come mighty close to uh life sentence – with Mrs. Cromwell – but the scheming reverend was spared from that cruel an' unusual punishment by uh benevolent Providence who sent an eagle-eyed Duluth police officer to investigate the New Boonies Barrel Bust, which Grimly's arrest come t' be knowed as. The observant lawman observed the Reverend and his Lady cantering down Main Street in uh open carriage and wreck-on-I-zed the buggy's female occupant as Mil-licent Stone, uh Duluth Lady of the Night, what married up old geezers an' gottum t' leave her their money.

After leavin' prison, Grimly Thudmunson never come back, an'

Grover was near laughed right outta New Boonies. But, they never did take his hand-tinted daguerreotype down; it's still hangin' in the lobby of The New Boonies Righteous Shepherds Lodge buildin', captioned: "Vigilance against Sin is Virtue." Seems he didn't vigilate hard enough.

Whenever Ah think on those two old coots con-testin' over that there Duluth Lady, I think Retribution got two birds with one (Millicent) stone.

54

Uh Change of Heart

Ah got me some good news that, at first, I thought could be bad news. Mr. Foreman was still in his office last night when Ah punched in fer mah watchin' shift. He called me in an' says, "OK, now. Sit down, Mudge, let's have a little talk." Mah heart skipped uh beat er so on account Ah was worried "a little talk" might be the one where they tells ya how sorry they is, but they gotta cut back on overhead an' you's the one that's over their head, so here's yer last paycheck, goodbye. Instead, Mr. Foreman says, "OK now. Mudge, you're doing a great job; look for a dollar an hour raise on your next check."

"Gee, thanks, Mr. Foreman."

"We've got our eye on you now . . . always looking for supervisors, OK?"

Ah been watchin' fer Amalgamated Associates real good, ever since I got here, an' I ain't never seen nothin' looked like uh supervisor. Still, Ah played along. "That sounds real great, sir, thanks again."

"OK now. We've racked up enough time on the clock for our little chit-chat." He give uh sort of phony laugh. "It's back to work now, OK? You don't want t' be late on your clocking-in rounds . . . would ruin your record."

"You bet, OK, sir." I was real relieved. I'll bet there warn't uh supervisor within uh hundred miles, so I don't have t' worry none about gettin' pro moated off my watchin' job soz Ah can't do writin' every night. An' right now, I gotta write uh storm of stuff on account of MerryMae sent some of mah stories t' uh book publishin' outfit called Big Fithe Press. It were uh nice surprise when they sent uh letter back sayin' they'd like t' see more of mah writin'.

MerryMae asked me how Ah gits the ideas fer mah writin' an' Ah told her they just come t' inside mah head, especially just after I finished up on uh story, sorta like a long thread. Like the time Ah didn't notice when I caught uh loose string of yarn from my mitten onta uh nail stickin' outa cousin Wigglesword's barn door an' durned if it didn't pull that mitt offen mah hand inta one long string – fer me, story writin' is just one long string . . . although it don't make mah hand near so cold as unravelin' uh mitten. An' some recent stories Ah writ, like how Andrew Titus an' LukeSimon Mathew's got their comeuppance in old Harden Steel's courtroom, reminds me of how durn tricky that judge was. Ya didn't see eye t' eye with him, he'd make ya; take the case of troublemakin' bully Elijah Biggleton, who hated his neighbor so bad he tried t' hire uh assininator t' do 'im in.

———————◆———————

Hear tell, near everybody in Huns Point Avoided Elijah Biggleton on account he was big as uh barn an' meaner than uh wet bobcat. He could clear out uh saloon about as quick as somebody shoutin', "Free whisky across the street."

He lived on uh sliver of farmland just on the edge of Huns Point and had but a single neighbor, the unfortunate Mr. Lloyd Everett. Unfortunate on account of livin' next t' uh man what took pleasure in makin' life miserable fer other folks, an' double unfortunate because he was the kinda man that looked for good in all men. But Ah guess nobody's eyesight was good enough t' see much good in Elijah Biggleton. Near everbody in Huns Point knowed how Elijah Biggleton loathed his neighbor. Guess it started when Old Everett wouldn't let his daughter,

Lloyette, take up with Biggleton, and the bully never fergive er fergot, just hated Mr. Everett more every day.

Over the years, Elijah knocked down Mr. Everett's fences, stole uh cow an' uh couple of pigs, tromped his horse through the Everett's vegatable garden, shot his dog, an' terrified his family. Through all this, Mr. Everett was calm and forgiving, which simply goaded the frightful monster inta bigger an' bigger intimidations. Finally, however, the placid peacemaker had t' seek the protection of the law, on account of rumor got around that Biggleton had hired a saloon acquaintance t' cut Everett's throat.

Turns out that there was such buzzin' an' gossip about Biggleton wantin' Everett D-ceased that the potential assassin lost his nerve an' went t' the cops. It weren't long after that, the terror of Huns Point wuz gittin' his dinner served in uh cell what had bars that even he couldn't clear out.

Seizing the opportunity to rid the community of bully Biggleton, the Wet County Attorney indicted the town terror fer near every crime on the books except impersonatin' Santa Claus – official dumb wuz gonna git this guy on somethin'! Nobody really had t' worry about that on account of what Elijah Biggleton got, was a trial before Judge Harden Steel, without uh doubt, the toughest judge since Torquemada.

Judge Steel had uh habit of wavin' lawyers aside an' directly questioning both witnesses an' accused in his court. He hated "expert" witnesses, referrin' to um as "paid liars blessed by uh naïve court system." Uh feller come inta the Judge's court claimin' he was uh expert on horse-drawn implements; the case involved traces what broke causin' uh run-a-way team t' commit damage of property. Judge Steel questioned the expert on his general knowledge of harness fittings and teams and inquired how the whippletrees became tangled so as to spook the runaways. The "expert," a reporter from a big city newspaper doing uh "undercover" story on Wet county judicial practices, an' aware of Judge Steel's reputation as a sly and devious martinet, decided to do a little deviousing of his own, an' replied, "You can't fool me with a trick question, Your Honor. Whippletrees are a species of spruce indigenous to Siberia." Said reporter learned all about whippletrees. His six-month sentence, for "false representations [of expertise] to the court," was as a "shovel-hand" at the Huns Point Fire and Police Stables.

Well, ya coulda been blind as Justice, but ya always knowed when ya wuz in Judge Steel's courtroom on account of he started every session with the same words: "Justice may be blind, but that don't mean she gotta be stupid. . . ." He'd rap his gavel hard enough t' beat down crime fer uh cent-chur-E or so.

". . . Court's in session!" Thar warn't no "Hear yee, hear yee" baloney.

The case of People vs. Biggleton was no exception. "Mr. District Attorney, call your first witness."

Ernie Inarsson shuffled to the witness box like he was strugglin' against an in-visible rope tied t' his waist. The rope almost pulled him to a stop when he glanced at Biggleton.

"Get uh move on," said the Judge.

Like he was grateful to be directed, Earnie slouched to the witness stand, was sworn to truthfulness, and recited his full name, age, and address.

District Attorney Beater got right down t' business. "Now, Mr. Inarsson, you are here today of your own volition?"

Earnie appeared somewhat dazed. "Mah what?"

"Your free will. You came here voluntarily."

"If I were the counsel for defense, I'd be on my feet, objecting to you leading the witness," broke in Judge Steel. He glared at Nerdon Dagget. "Just stay seated, counselor, the court's done your work for you."

Both Dagget and the DA seemed shocked at the rebuke from the bench. Neither spoke for a moment, giving Earnie Inarsson an opening to spring his own well-prepared defense.

"It ain't no crime t' listen . . . even . . ."

The star witness was interrupted by the DA. "Yes, yes, let me rephrase . . . Have you come to this court of you own free will, Mr. In-

168

arsson?"

"It ain't no crime t' listen . . . even t' uh criminal like Elijah!"

Defense attorney Dagget rose to the occasion. "Object . . . non-responsive and presenting facts not in evidence, your Honor."

"Sit down, Nerdon, your turn will get here." He nodded at the re-composed DA.

"Did you come here as a law abiding citizen, Ernie?"

"I got uh paper, but it ain't no crime t' listen . . . even t' uh . . ."

The Judge banged his gavel. "Mr. Beater, ain't you gone over this with 'im?"

"Sure have, Judge, but I think he's still scared of being implicated."

"Come on up t' the bench, Mr. Beater."

There followed a conversation, some might say monologue, at the bench. The DA's head bobbed up an' down like he was tryin' t' dislodge somethin' nasty from his throat and somewhat smiled when His Honor finished up, which some that were sittin' close have reported the Judge sayin', "And don't let that jackass waste any more of the court's time."

Mr. Beater addressed the witness in his best no-nonsense voice. "Earnie, you've been granted immunity from any charge arising from this case, remember?"

"Yes, sir, Mr. Beater . . . just wanna make sure you know it ain't no crime t' listen."

"We both agree on that, Ernie, now, please tell the court what the defendant asked of you."

"He said I was t' cut the . . . the . . . kin I . . . should I use Elijah's swear words, do I say um here?"

"Yes," said the DA, "or a representation, like SOB . . . and point out, for the court, who said the words to you."

"He did," said the witness, who by now had warmed to his task and extended an accusing arm and somewhat wavering finger toward Mr. Biggleton. "He said, 'Cut the SOB's throat from ear t' ear.' Then he

169

said, 'Don't leave nothin' t' chance, keep cuttin' till his head goes, clean off.' "

Predictably, the onlookers gasped and whispered. Predictably, Judge Steel silenced the sibilant breech of decorum with several smart whacks of his gavel and pointed at the DA.

"And please tell the court why he expected you to participate in such a dastardly crime?"

"Because, he said iffin I didn't do it, he'd 'beat me inta uh pulp uh butcher couldn't see was human,' an' I believed him. He's the scariest guy I ever knowed."

"Your witness, Mr. Dagget."

The Defense attorney did his best t' whitewash his client's culpability, but it was uh little like suggestin' Mt. Everest ain't got no snow on top, everybody knowed different.

Judge Steel rolls' his eyes an' says, "Save uh little of the hearts an' flowers for the summation, counselor. Now, I wanna ask why? Mr. Biggleton, will you please explain to the court why you plotted your neighbor's demise?"

Dagget jumped to his feet. "Objection, 'plotting' is assuming facts not in . . ."

"Duly noted, Mr. Dagget, now, sit down, shut up, and do not interrupt me again, sir." He glanced at the defense table and his expression said, Have you ever seen a defense attorney plead for mercy from a long, long contempt citation? "Now, will the defendant kindly do me the honor of an answer?" He stared quizzically at Biggleton.

The meanest man in a hundred miles stared back D-fiant-lee, but finally withered before the glare of a man increasing mean distance tenfold. "I hated the SOB. He was a GD smarmy, goody two shoes . . . thought Lloyette was too good for me!"

"If I could persuade you to change your mind . . ."

"Nothin' could ever make me change my mind! I hope that simpering, SOB gets ate by pigs."

Judge Steel clearly didn't like interruptions, an' more than that, he didn't seem t' like that the defendant sorta challenged him. "Mr. Biggleton, if your sentence were adjusted, could I convince you to adjust your attitude toward your neighbor?"

"You can adjust about anythin' you want . . . an' I kin spit in yer eye, Judge. I hate that man an' I wanna see him dead . . . dead as uh doornail!"

The Judge said one word. "Summations!"

The attorney's sum-up words were noticeably brief, probably hardly noticed.

The jury rendered the expected verdict on all counts, and then sat to hear the Judge render his.

Judge Harden Steel cleared his throat and paused while absolute silence settled over the court assemblage. "Please stand for sentencing, Mr. Biggleton." The defendant awkwardly lumbered from his seat, but not too ungainly for uh fellow whose hands were cuffed behind him. "I have been examining your file, sir, and note that you are forty-four years of age, is that correct?" He glanced at the defendant expectantly. Biggleton's mouth remained closed and set; it was clear he was through talking. "Very well," said the Judge, "count one, for the crime of conspiracy to murder I hereby sentence you to forty-four years of hard labor in The Territorial Prison. Count two, for the crime of domestic terrorizing, namely, your neighbors, I hereby sentence you to twenty-two years of hard labor in The Territorial Prison. Count three, for the crime of terroristic threats, namely to Mr. Ernest Inarsson, I hereby sentence you to twenty-two years of hard labor in The Territorial Prison. Do you have a last statement, Mr. Biggleton?

The huge man surprised everyone as he growled, "I hate the SOB, nobody er nothin' will ever change my mind."

"Oh, dear, I was afraid of that Mr. Biggleton, and therefore add this addendum to your sentence. Count One shall run concurrent with Counts Two and Three, however Count Two and Count Three shall run consecutively. No parole is to be granted on any of the Counts. You may expect to be released a free man by your 88th birthday." The Judge paused to let the enormity of the sentence fill all the proper spaces in folk's thoughts. "However, in the interests of mercy, both from the court and your heart, I am adding an ameliorating stipulation, to wit: The court notes that the object of your criminal intent, namely, Mr. Everett, is presently eighty-four years of age, and seems to be in ordinary health for a man in that age category. Therefore, he may reasonably be expected to survive for what, well, who might dare to estimate. However, the Court orders that for each full year Mr. Everett shall survive, following this proceeding, fours years shall be reduced from each of your respective sentences. Should Mr. Everett survive but a mere five years, you might still look forward to a decent stretch of life. But, should it come to pass that your heretofore intransigent desire is fulfilled, to see this man's life immediately terminated, I say to you, happy 88th birthday, Mr. Biggleton."

Rumor had it that Elijah Biggleton found religion in prison, because every morning and every evening his knees found the floor of his cell as he prayed for the good health and well being of the man he once sought so ardently to kill . . . quite a change of heart.

55

From Heart Changin' t' Heart Breakin'

There was quite a few folks what said Judge Harden Steel didn't have no heart. On the other hand, hear tell, there was some that thought he might of. When Ah thinks back on all them stories what they tells about the Judge, an' some of his "punishment-fittin'-the-crime" sentences, I think on the story of old Olaf Rundstrom an' his neighbor Herbert Eriksson. Ole and Herbie owned adjacent farms, just uh couple of miles South of Wet Lake, an' seein' as they had growed up fishing an' playin' an' goin' clear through eight grade together, they was about as close as friends can get.

Herbie had a twisted scar startin' at his wrist and endin' with fingers of hard, white skin wrapping around his neck, from the time he helped put out a fire in Ole's barn, sorta balancin' the neighborly scales for the time Ole pulled out Herbie's oldest boy who had slipped into the icy, rushing Wet River one Spring. They was both decons in The German Lutheran Church, were steady partners in the Grange Whist Tournament, and brother Keepers of the Crook in the New Boonies Righteous Shepherds Lodge. Rumor had it that they was such good friends that they even called the other's Missus by their first names!

So, you can imagine the shock and disbelief when folks opened up the *Huns Point Herald* and saw that Olaf Rundstrom was jailed and awaiting trial for the Murder of Herbert Eriksson.

Ah put this here story together from talkin' to uh buncha New Boonies old timers and The Huns Point newspapers what was wrappin' up some family china that Aunt Thudalia never used. Frederick said this is writ in first person, but that ain't right on account of lots of other folks has wrote about Harden Steel before me. Why, Ah remembers plenty of writin' kom-mean-tarys on the Judge, right in New Boonies, especially in the Gents' Room at the Grand Saloon. Anyhow, Ah am takin' the liberty of pretendin' I'm uh mouse under the Judge's chair.

Judge Steel raps his gavel so hard that everybody in the courtroom sorta jumps, even us mice. The buzzing room stilled.

"...Court's in session! The People vs. Rundstrom....Who represents the people?"

The ritual question was answered by District Attorney Beater.

"...For the defense?"

"Nerdon Dagget, Your Honor."

The Judge turned to the Defendant, "Mr. Rundstrom, it's my understanding that you have waived your right to be heard by a jury of your peers, and elected the bench to adjudicate the facts in this matter, is that correct?"

The Defendant looked at the floor. "...I...I don't know about no benches er stuff...vass kinda thinkin' you'd do it, Judge."

"Relax Mr. Rundstrom, no benches. I'll hear the case and make the calls...OK?"

"Yeah...sure...uh, uh, Yer Honor."

"Mr. Beater ... please limit your opening statement to the charge and a very short summary...if you must."

District Attorney Beater understood that despite imminent elections, toleration for campaigning in Judge Steel's courtroom was limited to nil. "The Defendant is charged with Second Degree Murder, Your Honor. The people will show that he killed his neighbor in a fit of ra . . ."

Dagget sprang to his feet. "Objection . . . supposition stated as fact, Your Honor."

"Duly noted. You are aware, are you not, Mr. Dagget, that the District Attorny is allowed to state his case? Please sit down, Sir. And permit me to go on record . . . I would prefer that you remain seated unless presenting your case from the bar. Far from assigining more credence to assertions made while bounding about the courtroom, being only human, I am likely to discount arguments in proportion to their accompaniment of circus theatrics. . . .

" . . . Are you finished, Mr. Beater?" Without waiting for the obligatory, "Yes, Your Honor," the impatient jurist called on the Defense.

Attorney Dagget claimed his client was innocent by virtue of circumstance, ". . . A tragic accident . . . an' I'll save my statement for summation."

"Mr. Beater, call your first witness."

Byron Gutknecht was the closest official Wet County had to a detective. He had hidden behind his share of road signs in the County's quest to apprehend speeding vehicles (while adding to administrative coffers), directed traffic from fairs to funerals, broken up countless alcoholic disagreements in Wet County's watering holes, and for more years than most could remember, played Santa Claus in the Annual Huns Point School Pagent. After being sworn to truthfulness, he recited his name, carefully spelling it for the clerk of court, and at the District Attorney's prompting, identified the murder weapon; "That's it all right . . . kin tell because I carved my initials inta it, right there." He pointed to fresh scratches on the evidence. The defense accepted his testimony without challenge or question.

The murder weapon was duly recorded as Exhibit #1 and carefully sequestered from loss or damage, being plopped onto the edge of the clerk's desk. The DA busily wiped his fingers and said, "For the record, Your Honor, I will describe the *telum homicidiale.* . . ."

"Oh for gosh sakes Beater, you're as blind as Justice. Can't you see there's no jury to impress? Now get on with it."

"Of course, Your Honor. The deceased suffered a fatal brain injury after being struck with Exhibit Number One. To wit: a wooden pail of about two gallon capacity constructed from oaken staves and fitted with a handle of rope. . . . It held the axle grease that both the defendant and victim were using at the time of the murder."

Nerdon Dagget mumbled, "uhmm . . . accident."

Judge Steel glanced at the defense attorney; his eyebrows lifted, as though surprised to see attorney Dagget.

The prosecutor ignored the breech of decorum, and appeared to be warming up for a longer dissertation but fell silent as Judge Steel broke in. "Thank you, Mr. Beater. Now, let's hear from the defense. . . ." His tone radiated sarcasm. "According to conventional jurisprudence."

"My client is innocent, Your Honor. The entire incident was an accident."

"You keep repeating that like a mantra, Mr. Dagget. Please bear in mind that I am the finder of facts in this case; so far, I have no factual evidence to support innocence . . . or guilt."

"We admit he done it. But it was unintentional . . . completely unintentional. . . . Actually, Your Honor, we rest our case."

Judge Steel rolled his eyes, so obvious that even us mice on the floor could see 'im do it. Then, he said, "Mr. Rundstrom, please step to the bar."

Ole stood and looked around but he didn't see no bar, and there warn't no bartender to point it out. So, he just stood by the little railing that run in front of the high platform where the Judge sat.

"Thank you, Sir. Now, do you admit that you caused the death of Mr. Eriksson?"

"Ye-aah."

"Please tell the court how that happened."

"I picked up the grease bucket an just clumped 'im a mite."

"And why did you do that."

"Oh, I had to Judge."

"Listen to me, Ole, Why did you have to 'clump' your friend?"

"It vass an emergency."

Judge Steel closed his eyes and shook his head. Along with Olaf Rundstrom, His Honor's patience was obviously on trial. Mustering an even voice, he said, "Just start from the beginning, Mr. Rundstrom, tell us what happened . . . in your own words."

Ole stared at the berobed man, probably wondering in whose words, if not his own, might he relate the tragedy. "Vell, sir, it vass like dis: it vass a couple of months ago, ya know, and I vass just about to cut hay offen my back forty . . . as I recall, it had rained some that night and it vass a real pretty morning, ya know, how the sun makes the dew look like a touwsun dimonds winking from the grass. . . . Vell, I'd finished up the milking, which vass a little early because both Agnes and Gunda vass dry . . . which reminds me, I gotta get Sig Vigglesvord's bull over to my place. . . ."

"Mr. Rundstrom . . ."

"Oh, ye-aah, Yer Honor . . . vell, I'd finished up the milking and come back t' da house fer breakfast and vass just finishing up a bowl of Wheaties® . . . no, no, maybe it vass oatmeal that morning. I like Wheaties® but sometimes the Missus fixes oatmeal. . . . She says, 'Ole, ya gotta have food that sticks to yer ribs,' and . . ."

His Honor lightly tapped the gavel. Ole noticed and sort of came back on point.

"Yes sir, Yer Honor. I vass right in the middle of my oatmeal when Herbie come by . . ."

Judge Steel broke in. "Just for the record, Mr. Rundstrom, by 'Herbie,' are you referring to the decedent, Mr. Herbert Eriksson?"

"Yes sir, Yer Honor, sir. Herbie sure vass decent . . . vass gonna help me get the hay crop cut and into the barn before vee got more rain."

"Then why would you 'clump' such a 'decent' man?"

"I vass just coming to dat part, Yer Honor. I already told ya I vass in the middle of my cereal an Herbie could see that I wasn't done yet so he asks me if dere vass anything he could do to help out while I vass still eating. I says, 'Oh, yeah. The hay wagon is still up on blocks because I gotta grease the axles; ya can start on dat.' So Herbie leaves to do dat and I'd just about finished up when I looks out the window and seen him by the back of the wagon. He had the grease bucket in one hand and the big brush in the other. He vass all set to slather grease onto the back axle.

Vell, I jumped up so fast my chair tipped over but I just didn't pay no attention to that an I run out the door without even taking my breakfast bib off, and waved my hands and shouted like crazy to get Herbie's attention. Tank goodness, I caught him just in time. He sets the grease pail down and says, "What's the matter, Ole, why are ya shouting?" I snatches up the grease bucket, so he couldn't get at it and says, "I had to stop ya, Herbie. I seen ya just about to grease the axle there . . . but you can't do dat, it's the back axle, an I always grease the front axle first."

"Well," says Herbie, "I always grease the back axle first."

"And I'm telling you, here on my place, we grease the front axle first."

"Well, over t' my place, vee grease da back axle first!"

"Front axle!"

"Back axle!"

"Front axle!"

"He was still holding the brush full of grease and raised his hand like he was gonna smear a dollop onta the back axle. I still hadda hold of the bucket, and it was sorta natural to just give him a clump . . . I had to, Your Honor."

"And why did you have to?"

"If I hadn't clumped 'im, the durn fool woulda greased the back axle first!"

His Honor mulled the Defendant's testimony for about ten seconds and says, "Mr. Rundstrom, the court concurs with the bill of indictment and finds you guilty as charged."

Have you anything further to say before I pronounce the sentence?"

"No . . . I guess not, Your Honor," and added in a small voice, "but he shoulda never tried t' do the back one first."

Judge Steel permitted himself a highly audible and un-judge-like sigh, he squeezed shut his eyes, accompanied with a slight shake of the head, and said, "Olaf Klemens Rundstrom, I hereby sentence you to twenty years imprisonment at hard labor." He then paused.

The onlookers were aghast. The courtroom buzzed in shocked disbelief. In those days, many familys went hungry when a Papa got sent t' the hoosegow and everyone knew that Herbie's death wasn't intentional. How could the judge be so cruel? You couldn't give a Wet County farm away, let alone sell one. How could the four Eriksson and five Rundstrom kids eat? The indignant gallery vented its displeasure in not overly subtle whispers and sour looks toward the bench. Yet, uncharacteristically, as some have observed, the Judge refrained from any admonishment, permitting the courtroom's commentary on his justice to run out of steam.

When decorum was reestablished, Judge Steel continued. "Ole, you are hereby remanded to the joint custody of Adelade Rundstrom and Constance Eriksson. You will serve out your sentence by working both farmsteads, your own and Mrs. Eriksson's, without any additional compensated help."

Puzzlement covered the convicted man's face.

"That means," said the Judge, "you are to receive no hired help. You must work both the farms by yourself. . . . You do recall I said 'hard labor'?"

Ole nodded.

"Any or all income from the farms will be divided equally between your wife, Adelade and Mrs. Eriksson. And one more detail.

You are hereby required to grease all County trucks, front-end loaders, graders, snowplows, and rolling stock once a month at the County machine shed under the supervision of Maintenance Manager, Ski Sorenson. He will see to it that you always begin your greasing duties at the back of each vehicle. You will receive general supervision by the county parole officer, who will monitor your compliance with all these sentencing conditions. . . . Should you fail . . ." The ominous statement remained incomplete, but the implication was clear. Judge Steel paused, addressing his clerk. "Who's our new parole officer, Audrey?"

"It's just a part-time job, and I think the County Board got that position on hold for now, Judge . . . actually since this whole case started."

"And why is that?"

"They only had one applicant. He applied last year, but before they could approve him, this case come up."

"Don't beat around the bush like that, Audrey. Who the heck is it?"

"Olaf Rundstrom."

56

FAIR OR NOT, THEY TOOK UH LICKIN'

I guess they don't make judges like Harden Steel no more, which I suppose some is grateful for. Aunt Thudalia used t' say if they had more judges like Harden Steel, there wouldn't be half the stealing an' stuff. Though some said it was really Judge Steel who stole the people's fun and not the mayor of Millerton, who got the blame.

Aunt Thudalia talked a lot about the Great Depression. Actually, Ah guess there warn't too much great about it except folks kinda learned t' use their injun-ooity, instead of a lot of money, t' have a good time. Like the way the County Fair Board come up with a pretty cheap way to build attendance.

They dug a post hole by the main gate and set a husky fence post in it with uh silver dollar stuck inta the top. It was tall enough so a driver sittin' in a car had to reach up, over their head, to feel the coin on top. They couldn't see the dollar, just feel it, and guess if it were heads or tails. The gatekeeper would flip the coin and set it in the post for each driver so nobody knew what side it was until after it got felt. Following each guess, the attendant held a little mirror so, without getting out of the car, the driver could see the coin. A correct guess, and the carload passed free, a wrong guess, and everybody in the car had t' pay an extra dollar over the regular admission.

Turned out that was a lotta fun and after the first year, the County Fair Board made enough extra money soz they could fix the grandstand and the hog pens with funds left over to gravel and grade the road goin' inta the grounds. But, wouldn't ya know it, an a-nonymous some-one, supposedly acting on behalf of The Ladies Augzillery to the New Boonies Righteous Shepherds Lodge, suggested that the Silver Dollar Game amounted to gambling. And, as it was just before election time, County Attorney Beater was persuaded to bring the matter before Wet County's most stringent arbiter of justice, Judge Harden Steel.

Those folks who feared that the Silver Dollar Game might ravel the moral fabric of Wet County residents slumbered peacefully following Judge Steel's pronouncement: "The game is a blatant attempt to introduce gambling into our otherwise virtuous community."

Later, it was discovered that the push to eliminate the corruptive game originated not with the The Ladies Augzillery to the New Boonies Righteous Shepherds Lodge, but with the rival Fair Board over in Deertrack County, on account of their folks was spending money in Wet County. By then, our Fair Board had moved on to the Value of Money Contest.

No gambling. Each contestant paid a dollar to drive their tractor over a silver dollar and see if they could determine if it were heads or tails. Winners got a twelve page *Farmer's and Trapper's Almanac* and a ticket redeemable for a free ice cream cone. However, the Contest sorta fizzled on account of the Mayor of the County's smallest town, Millerton, population 17, was caught licking up the last of the three-gallon bucket that the contest winner's ice cream was stored in. Well, there went the contest!

That season, the County Fair Board had more debt than income. Subsequently, the road to the fairgrounds got no fresh gravel or grading. And, despite developing major leaks, the grandstand roof received no attention. Even the hog pens fell into shameful disrepair. In fact, Julius Johansson, a Wet County hog farmer who had won many blue ribbons at the fair, was heard to comment, "Them hog pens ain't fit fer uh Norwegian."

Just to clear the air, I think Mr. Johansson was Swedish.

57

Of Belts & Breakfasts

It's surprisin'. Uh while back, the first person Ah might ask fer help on uh writin' problem would of been Uncle Morton. Nowadays, I feel like Ahm sorta imposin' on uh matra moneyed couple. Ah see Mort down t' the Town Tavern on an occasional Thursday evening, which is one of mah night's off, but since cuttin' down on Leinenkugelin', even that ain't much. So, when the stories slowed up comin' t' mah head, I talked t' Socrates about it. He said the newspapers might gimme uh in-spire-A-shun, but maybe I should try MerryMae an' Chrys. Good idea. I X-plained to mah neighbors that Ah kinda come t' the end of mah mitten string – of writin' ideas. We talked it over fer quite uh while but come up dry.

The next day MerryMae gimme uh call an' says, "After you left, I got to talking about your writer's block with Chrys, and he came up with a suggestion that might help."

Well, Ahm too old fer blocks an' such, but Ah just let that pass. "What's his idea?"

"Chrys thought you might take a few days off and go up t' New Boonies for a visit, see how the renter is treating your house, drive around a little. . . . Something may come to you. . . . Very least, you can just rest your mind, maybe get a fresh perspective."

"Gee, thanks . . . an' thank Chrys fer me. Bye, now." The more

Ah thought on it, the better the idea sounded. An', when Ah asked Mr. Foreman about takin' uh few days off he OK'd me fer three days of mah vacation; that, with mah two night break gimme a good spell t' git inta uh New Boonies frame t' mah mind.

First thing Ah done when Ah got t' New Boonies wuz park by the square an' walk over t' The Rock; the grass needed uh little mowin, but it was bare dirt where folks musta stood and read the plaque. It's sorta pecu-liar, but when Ah left, I don't recall even noticin' the size of Old Charlie's cussin' stone . . . just always thought of it as bein' real big, like way over mah head. Ahm pretty sure that old stone didn't shrink none but nowadays it don't come no higher than mah shoulder.

Ah remembers playin' tag an' such, hiding behind Charlie an' Dan's monument. Another thing come t' mind, about how uh corner of it kinda stuck out inta the way of projectin' the Summertime Saturday night movie what New Boonies merchants used t' put on t' git folks inta town. Felix the Cat or Rudolph Valentino would have t' fight their way through about uh zillion moths hoverin' an' flittin' through the projector beam, t' git to the wrinkled sheet hanging on the bandstand. Them wuz good times. I remember one Saturday night, Mr. Howard Marshall, the man what come back from the gold minin' in Alaska with uh woolly mammoth's tooth, give both me an' Timmy Thudmunson uh nickel t' buy an ice cream cone. Boy, Mr. Marshall musta got really gener-ossified up t' them gold mines; nobody else we ever heard of ever give money away in New Boonies.

Ah walked over t' the bandstand, which was also uh lot littler than Ah recollected. Never would fit more than three er four mew-zish-huns, except no sousaphone could git on with nobody else. It needed paint real bad an' some of the railing an' about half the slats formin' its skirt was missin'; boy, the pathetic little eyesore shoulda got tore down long ago. Well, I sure didn't git no idea fer uh story outta the park . . .

fact is, though Ah can't figure why, I come away feelin' uh little sad.

Next stop was Aunt Thudalia's house; technically, it's mine now, but I just natural think of it as mah Aunt's. Pulled inta the driveway an didn't see no lady inna long dress an' big sunbonnet hoein' in the garden. Of course, I knowed better, but them kinda ideas is hard t' let go of. Instead, Matilda Zimmermann come outta the back door yoohooin' about uh cup of tea. We went inside an' set uh spell. I asked Tildy if there was anything needin' fixin' an' she said LeRoy Jasper, from down the road, had come over in the fall an' put up some electric ice meltin' cables on the back roof, t' keep an ice dam from makin leaks, like last year.

"I'd be obliged if ya was t' pay fer them, Mudge. LeRoy said he'd wait till you come up an' give ya uh bill, if yer OK on payin' it."

"Well of course Ah am. . . . Anythin' else?"

"We might have t' deepen the well next year. Don't know where the water's goin'. . . . Had us an ordinary winter snow, and I suppose the rain was regular this spring but the paper says the whole watertable is getting used . . . must be them big mines an' stuff. Anyway, if your heading up to Huns Point you'll see . . . some of the rock on the ford is dry.

"Just do whatever needs doin', Tildy. . . . Wantcha t' be comfortable here."

I am, Mudge. Never thought I would be. . . . Problem was, our place was just too big for me t' run on my own. . . . Renters don't seem t' see things need doin', not that I'm one uh those kind! Never gave Cecil credit for how hard he worked around that farm, broke my heart, but selling it was a blessing . . . and it never come to me how much I missed Cese . . . but we go on . . . secretaryin' for the Mayor is a lifesaver, get t' meet folks all the time . . . an' yes, I'm real comfortable . . . but land! I'm going on so . . . more tea?"

"Thank ya, Tildy, but ya gimme uh idea when ya mentioned the ford . . . 'stead of goin' back home, think I'll head on up t' Huns Point."

"Mercy! It's almost dark out, Mudge. You just stay here tonight, in your old room. . . . Don't know what you can do up there on a Sunday, but at least you can leave tomorrow morning with uh good break-fast under your belt."

58

Discovery Can Be Unbearable

Didn't sleep real good in mah old room. Besides, it ain't my room no more. Tildy's grandson Roger, Ahm guessin' he's goin' on about twelve, stays here once in a while. He's got the walls covered with big posters of star trekkin' fellas and super guys in fancy uniforms speeding faster un bullets an' spiderin' from tall buildin's an' such. There was bright moonlight and a fee-row-shush wind an' Ah kept wakin' up from imaginin' me an' one of them spiderin' guys gettin' all crashed up after drivin' off the top of some tall skyscrapin' tower in uh bat-mo-bile.

In spite of them sleep inner-ruptions, I really enjoyed stuffin' uh whoppin' breakfast under mah belt, an' after me an' Tildy finished up all the thanks fer breakfast an' thanks fer stopping-by politeness, Ah headed up toward Huns Point. Then uh pecu-liar car thing overcome mah drivin; like the Buick had it's own mind under the hood there, instead of goin' back t' New Boonies the durn car turned onta Petersen Road an' before I really thought on it, Ah was on County Road #40, headin' out t' Highland Corners. Ah don't remember uh thing about that drive, wuz kinda like bein' hip-no-tyzed.

I parked in the shade of the popple grove and just sat, fer uh long spell. Funny, as uh boy, Ah come here with Aunt Thudalia many, many times an it was sorta uh chore, t' just wait while she was doin' her rememberin'; it wuz sure different this time. I tried t' git some ideas fer somethin' t' write in uh story, but didn't feel nothin' but powerful sadness, in fact, the whole durn visit has made me sad. Time was, I'd chase away discouragin' with uh visit t' The Grand, but Ah just ain't in the mood fer Leinenkkugelin'. I truly miss Aunt Thudalia an' I don't think Mort an' me is ever gonna be real pals again; that's when Ah noticed Ah been cryin, feelin' sorry fer mahself an cryin' like uh baby.

"You can't really go back, you have . . ."

"Well, I knows that, Miss Smallermann, you . . ."

Ah quit snivelin' an' talking t' ghosts, but I did get an idea. I couldn't really do nothin' in Huns Point on uh Sunday so Ah figured Ahd go back to her "orchard" an' visit Aunt Thudalia's grave, and then go on up an stop by Miss Smallermann's, could do both this afternoon. Ah did, an' then stayed overnight at Huns Point Haven, uh motel us kids used t' call Huns Point Heaven.

Was the summer I finally gradge-U-A-ted outta high school when Ah stayed there one night with Grace Thudmunson. We didn't do nothin' but drink beer and just talk. Bless Aunt Thudalia, she were the only one what believed the "just talk." Ah think Grace's daddy woulda shot me if he had got the chance; eventually, he calmed down, but it kinda ruined future true romancin' with Grace.

Monday mornin' Ah went on over t' the Point Professional Building, an' after uh short wait in his fancy waitin' place, Mr. Thudmunson comes outta his even fancier office an invites me in.

"Nice to see you, Mudge. Is this business or social?"

"Well, Mr. Thudmunson, ya is always so friendly an' social, but it might be business."

Mr. Thudmunson makes uh little mark on his desk calendar and says, "I'm all ears, Mudge, what 'might be business?' "

"Ah been givin' lots of thought lately t' mah Aunt an' Mr. Johnny Windsong. An' it ain't that I want nothing, Ahm more un grateful fer what come mah way, but when you an' me an Aunt Thudalia was first talkin', I seem t' remember you mentionin' somethin' about uh packin' case stored in yer . . . yer, well, Ah don't remember where ya stored it

190

but if ya still got it, Ah thought it coulda been somethin' mah Aunt mighta set some store in."

"By golly, that completely slipped my mind. I apologize, Mudge. . . ."

"There's no need t' . . ."

"No, no . . . very unprofessional of me. No excuse . . . maybe I was a little hung up on your Aunt's refusal . . . never had that happen before. Anyway, let's go down together and have a look."

"Down" to "have a look" was uh ride t' the basement in an elevator what had blankets hangin' on the sides.

"Sorry we have to take the freight elevator, but the others don't go down to the lowest level . . . security." The door opened to uh big hallway with rooms runnin' along the sides. "You could store gold down here, Mudge, look there, cameras monitor this area day and night."

I didn't say nothin' on how Amalgamated Associates warehouses git robbed once in uh while, even with guys like me watchin' right in um. Mr. Thudmunson stops by uh door, which I see is metal clad, and turns the little wheels on uh combination lock built right inta the door. "Boy, that's uh pretty slick lookin' little lock."

"Like I said, this place is a regular junior Fort Knox."

"Oh, Ah wasn't knockin' the security here. . . ."

Mah lawyer gits that funny look folks sometimes git. Could be there ain't enough good air down here on account of Mr. Thudmunson sorta shakes his head like he's clearin' it. "There it is," he says, "just a packing case with 'fragile' stickers, but it's built like a church! . . . And darn near as big."

It wuz big, maybe nine feet tall and some four foot square, takin' up uh whole corner.

"Smells like some sorta cedar wood . . . an' got uh super big door, . . . an' would ya believe it? It's gotta lock!"

"Mr. Windsong sent along the key . . . had it in my desk all this time. Must apologize again, Mudge . . . completely slipped my mind. Here, the key is yours. You want to open it up in private?"

191

"Why, heck, no." I turned the key and the crate door opened easy as uh book cover. I could tell Pilfer hadn't opened the thing before, the way he snorted, "Holy smoke!"

"My gosh!" Uh huge, coppery colored, standing grizzly bear was starin' at me. An' though its bright brown eyes wuz just glass, Ah could swear Ah felt um measurin' me fer dinner.

59

Discovin' What Is Easy, Discovin' Why Ain't

When Ah got back home, Ah didn't know if Ah had something t' write about er not. There must be uh story in that there bear Johnny Windsong sent t' Aunt Thudalia, but durned if Ah kin figure what. Why in tarnation would he send her uh stuffed bear . . . an' as big as uh house t' boot? An' was them funny scratches just decoration er nothin'? Someday, maybe Ah'll write uh letter up t' Dale Windsong . . . see if maybe that bear had got some special meanin' t' Johnny Windsong.

Mr. Thudmunson was real nice about lettin' me keep on storin' mah monsterosity bear in his security place. Before I left, he made uh pretty good suggestion: "Why don't we throw in a handful of mothballs, just as a precaution."

"Sounds like uh good idea t' me, I'll do it, an' take me one more look-see at old bruin."

Ah went t' uh hardware store uh couple blocks from the Point Professional Building an' bought uh bag what said "para-dichlorobenzene," which musta been a real good deal on account of there was lots more than uh pair of um. Then Ah come back, took that special elevator with the blankets down t' mah bear and emptied the bag. When Ah went t' close up the door, Ah seen some scratches on the inside of the door, that Ah hadn't noticed before. There was three little vertical grooves with uh faint dug-in line on the top an' on the bottom of um. Ah wondered if it mighta been some secret message only Aunt Thudalia woulda knowed about. On the other hand, maybe it was just some way to mark the door planks.

Ah went back t' say goodbye t' Mr. Thudmunson an' thank 'im again fer safekeepin' the big critter.

"He's OK there as long as you want. And, by the way, I looked over the file and your first partnership distribution . . . from the saloon. It's due next month . . . Big Nugget Saloon. Maybe your furry giant has some connection to the saloon."

"What's the saloon like, Mr. Windsong ever say?"

"My only communication from John Windsong was his letter that I read to you and your Aunt. Oh, and he wrote a couple of lines at the bottom of a bank draft, said he hoped it was big enough to cover my fees and expenses."

"And was it big enough?"

"Enough so you'll never get a bill from me, on this matter."

◆

Talkin' the bear mystery over with Socrates was uh good idea on account of he suggested Ah call Frederick, the writer, t' see if he could help me make some sorta story outta Old Bruin.

Frederick said he'd try an' help but he wanted me t' A-tend some meetin' of uh writin' oufit: the Mini Tropolis Writers Workbench. They's writin' folks what give critty sizims of writin'. He said, "They're good folks, Mudge, even though some of them are a little weird."

Well, Ah went an it were uh con-fusing X-perience. They said Ah used too many words like add verbs an such. Of course, Ah could subtract um outta the writin' except Ah don't know what uh verb is. Uh lady talked about mah writin', fer what seemed forever, an' says I used too many run on sentences, which is another thing I ain't familiar with.

Like ending uh sentence with uh proposition. But the thing got me sorta riled wuz when uh fella said mah participle was danglin'. Well, he plum drove inta the ditch there, on account Ah would never do no such thing in public. Frederick was right, they was good an' weird.

When Ah met Frederick fer coffee, Ah told him Ah didn't think I was ready fer them fancy Workbench folks again real soon.

"That's probably reciprocal, Mudge."

Once in uh while, Ah think Frederick took Mort lessons on account of they both talk them big funny words. Anyways, we talked over the bear thing and come t' the con-collusion that uh story about Old Bruin would benefit from some details on Johnny and Aunt Thudalia. All Ah really knowed is that when Ah was uh kid, me an' Aunt Thudalia wuz regular goin' out t' Highland Corners where she would set an' remember Johnny.

"Who do you know that might know something of their relationship.?"

"Only one Ah kin think of is mah Uncle Mort. He's Aunt Thudalia's brother, but she was twenty years older un him."

"It's a start, Mudge, why don't you give it a try. . . . You can never tell what you'll discover."

60

Discovin' Can Be Disappointin'

When Ah called Mort t' ask him what he knowed about Aunt Thudalia and Johnny Windsong, what might explain somethin' about the bear, he says, "Not much. Think I'd just started going up to Huns Point (for school) when Windsong left, for . . . wherever he went."

"Alaska."

"I do remember he whittled a slingshot for me, nice fellow, too bad he and Thuddy never . . . got together."

"Nothin' else ya kin tell me?"

"Not about Thuddy and Windsong, but I've got some news. . . . We're going to California, and from now on I'm full Professor Wigglesword."

"Oh! Gosh . . . that's . . . uh . . . great, Mort." I felt like someone had punched me right in the stomach. "Misty OK on it?"

"Oh, yeah. She and Minerva had a big 'blow-up.' She's done with the Sippers. Matter of fact, she's already got a gig lined up for when we get there . . . plenty of voice ensembles in those college towns, and marching too, understand that protest movements are really flourishing out there." He sounded so happy when he said that.

"When ya leavin'?"

"End of the month, didn't want t' leave R & P in the lurch. 'Never burn a bridge.' . . . Remember that, Mudge."

"Ya, sure."

"Listen, Mudge . . . gotta go now, give you a call, just before we go. . . ."

Well, I didn't learn nothin' would shed light on the bear, but if I ever write uh book on discoverin' stuff, this will be the chapter on disappointment.

61

WHAT DO THEY CALL IT WHEN YOUR WORLD LEAVES WHILE YOU STAY BEHIND?

Finding out that Mort was gonna go way out t' California set me plum off mah feed. Ah usually try an write somethin' every night when Ahm doin' mah watchin' job, but I couldn't think of much else but how Ah'd miss Uncle Mort. Was feelin' powerful sorry fer mahself till Miss Smallermann come t' the rescue, "*You . . . have to go forward. . . .*" Forward seemed like uphill, but Ah concentrated on tryin' t' make uh story outta Old Bruin.

If Ah could just figure out why Mr. Windsong sent that nine-foot-tall, three Die-mention-ull rug t' uh lady he'd promised t' marry up with. If it was uh gift, it were sure pecu-liar. An' Ah couldn't believe it were uh apology. It musta been somethin' t' make up fer breakin' her heart. . . . He give her that Dieffenbachia plant more'n forty years ear-lier, which was plenty unusual then, but that durn bear was miles more than unusual. Uh wall woulda had t' git opened, an' then it woulda took uh con-struction crane to git the blame thing inta her house, an' the ceilings was too low . . . unless he was plum off his rocker, he oughta knowed that . . . but his letter didn't sound like he suffered no crazi-ness. It was one of them con-numb drums Mort talks about. Now, Ahm thinking on Mort again an' Ah gotta stop it on account of it's bringin' me sadness.

The next morning, when Ah got home, Socrates was more than his chatty self. Afore Ah could climb in bed he says, "A while back, you said you'd take me 'back home' if I wanted to go. . . . You remember that?"

"Well . . . Ah guess. Why ya ask?" Mah heart musta stopped, I knowed I didn't wanna hear his answer. I felt like Ah turned all them colors like Chrys does.

Socrates cocks his head an says, "Just testing."

Was dog tired, but still dreamin' of Old Bruin chasin' Mort an' Socrates up uh mountain when the phone ringin' wakes me up. I shoulda got up anyway because it was the middle of the afternoon. It was MerryMae, the fortune tellin' lady what lives next door.

"Hi, Mudge, can you come over for supper? . . . Of course, Socrates . . . about 5:30?"

"Oh, hi, MerryMae, sure that'd be nice. Kin Ah bring anything?"

"Just your appetite. . . . Bye."

Coffee an' raspberry pie topped off uh good stuffin' with somethin' MerryMae called beef struggle nuff, which sure weren't no struggle t' eat. She poured uh second cup of coffee an' says,

"Mudge, I've got a super opportunity, which I've already accepted. Everything about it fulfills my dreams . . . except leaving. I've grown really . . . attached . . . to you."

"Yer leavin' too?"

"What do mean, 'too'?"

"Oh, nothin' . . . where ya goin'?"

"Far away, Mudge. I'm going to be the curator of Grimoires at the Museum of Metaphysics."

"How far away?"

"Jamaica. . . . I've told you, when I adopted Chrys, I promised to love him and to keep him warm. Not easily done in Minnesota . . . but there's something else. . . . I . . . I'm not going t' beat-around-the-bush. . . . Can Socrates come with us?"

"Just testing." *Flunked that test!* "Ah guess . . . that's up t' Socrates."

Mah birdie friend didn't say nothin' – I don't know if he's told Chrys er MerryMae that he kin talk – sorta hung his head an' sat down next t' Chrys. Was an answer just as loud as words.

Some fellers would just go an' tie one on . . . but Ah don't think Ah could look uh Leinenkugel square in the eye. If I ever git uh book writ, this here will be the chapter on heartbreak . . . an Ah looked up uh better word: desolation.

62

YA GIT WHAT YA FIND, MAYBE

Lucky fer me, the last time I seen Frederick we'd arranged another meetin'.

"You look lower than a welldigger's heels, Mudge. Everything OK?"

"Oh, yeah . . . just still stuck on the Old Bruin thing, that's mah bear, that, an' everybody Ah knows seems t' be movin' t' the other side of the world."

"Sorry t' hear that, Mudge, but you know me, and I'm not going anywhere."

I felt uh little better. "That's 'forward.' "

"Didn't get that, Mudge."

"Oh, nothin', just talkin' to uh dead lady." Well, there it goes again. He sorta stares like he been struck dumb an' had t' think what he was gonna say next. Gosh, Ah can't figure why folks does that to me, it's plum puzzlin'.

"Oooo K. . . . Let's brainstorm about your bear . . . Old Bruin. . . . By the way, giving it a name is a good start . . . you've created a character."

We talked writin' ideas an' such, an' had us some lingonberry cake with our coffee; I think Frederick musta got some kinda loose head connection on account he ate his cake with his fork, again! It's amazin' that uh smart writin' guy like him don't know what his fingers is for. Still, he come up with uh great idea.

"Why don't you write your friend in Alaska . . . what's his name?"

"Dale."

"Why don't you write Dale, and see if he knows why his father sent a bear down here."

"Gosh, mah lawyer says Ahm due uh payment fer bein' uh partner, pretty soon. Ah kin ask him about it when I sends up uh thank-you letter."

The Big Nugget Saloon gotta be sorta small on account of I could spend mah share fer the past year in an afternoon an' still have time t' drive half way t' New Boonies. Lawyer Thudmunson said we could ask fer a four-mull accounting but I said, no, on account of I don't think Aunt Thudalia would of wanted t' question the honesty of Mr. Windsong's family.

I sent uh thank-you note, an' asked about the bear and Dale answered by sending me uh airplane ticket an' uh invite to come on up t' Desperation. Said she'd meet me at the Anchorage airport.

"I'll be waiting at your deplaning gate, and wearing a gold nugget the size of a thimble."

I guess they got uh lot of them nuggets up there, which is why, accordin' t' Aunt Thudalia, Mr. Windsong went t' begin with. Well, it didn't take long t' clear the vacation Ah had left with Mr. Foreman, an' then Ah was gittin' on uh big airplane what was also headed up t' Alaska.

Dammies! When we was comin' down fer uh landin' Ah could see there was near as much snow as we got in Minni Soota. They got mountains too; there was uh bunch of um ya could see from the airport. Gittin' off the airplane, I looked fer folks with gold nuggets but the only one I spotted was on uh necklace wore by uh good lookin' lady 'bout mah age, what had hair was black as coal. She smiled at me an' Ah kinda changed mah mind; she was real good lookin'. She stuck out her hand an' says, "You must be Mr. Wigglesword. Nice t' meet you. . . . Oh, I'm Dale, Dale Windsong."

Ah guess Ah was just starin' when it come t' me t' shake her hand , which was still stuck out t' me. "Uh . . . Ahm . . . uh, just call me Mudge . . . an' it's nice to meet you too . . . Dale?"

"Oh, that seems to fool most everybody, Toby . . . husband, never got used to it. . . ."

Ah couldn't uh told why, but at that moment mah heart sank down lower than somewheres south of Oregon.

". . . Dad gave me an unusual name. . . . I shortened it, but we can get to that later. For now, let's go eat, we've got a real little trek ahead of us."

Well, I sure found out what uh "little trek" was. First, uh cab ride to uh sort of uh kennel, leastwise there was plenty of dogs, an' then uh night an' uh day an' part of another night travelin', which warn't too bad except I ain't mentioned I was mostly travelin' in uh dogsled. Dale is as tough as she is good lookin'. We stopped fer sleepin' just once, otherwise, she either run behind or stood on the back sled runners fer all the way t' Desperation.

Actually, Desperation ain't much. Ah couldn't see it very good the night we got there, an' in spite of uh menagerie of stuffed critters all over the place, I practically passed out from mah travelin' tiredness, in one of the saloon's back rooms. The next mornin', after uh introductory sip of willow-tea with white lightening, in the bar out front, Dale introduced me around an' Ah saw what the town was like. There was four houses; each one of um were uh kinda business an' some had hughmungous signs an' with folks livin' behind their business. All of um had sled dogs tethered out back of their houses.

The saloon-sign on our place was some boards nailed over the front porch. It wuz sorta pecu-liar on account of it were painted with "Golden Bear" in white letters. They was painted over black letters what had said Big Nugget Saloon. When Ah asked her about it, Dale said she had just enough white paint to cover the Big Nugget words with Golden Bear, which was why the word saloon was still black. She even gimme uh X-planation about her sign:

"He had already passed on, but I did it for Dad. He was so . . . insistent, even thought maybe his mind was . . . uh . . . little . . . uh, wondering a bit. I don't think you could call it a conversation, but his last words . . . he kept saying 'No nugget, no nugget . . . golden bear.' They were his final words, actually . . . he raised right up, first time he'd sat in several days and said plain as I'm speaking to you now, 'I meant to tell you, it's not nuggets, Dale . . . golden bear!' It must have been too much . . . because he passed on right then."

There was uh bakery shop grocery store combination what also sold things like pails an' lanterns an' such; it's sign said: Best Baking this side of Gakona, so Ah s'pose it was pretty good eatin'. Gears Larson had the closest place, at least uh quarter mile away, who Dale says can build er fix practically anything; his house had four little paper signs in the front window sayin' "Carpenter," Mechanic," "Repairs," an' "& Guns To"; they was pretty much faded an' the paper looked kinda soggy an' in bad need of fixin'. He must be pretty reasonable; Dale says he repaired her balance scale an' only charged her uh couple of shots of lightening. The last place was a U.S. Post Office what serves folks livin' in what mah partner calls the "bush," run by an old-timer name uh Kincaid.

He took care of the saloon while Dale come t' pick me up. Guess he sorta baby-sits the place when she's away. Nice old fella . . . Ah asked if Kincaid was his first er last name an' he said, "Been sixty years since anybody called me anything else, so I reckon it don't matter." Ahm learnin' that's how folks seems t' git along so good here, they's pretty relaxed on matterin'.

Ah didn't bother Dale none on why her Daddy sent uh bear

down t' Aunt Thudalia, figurin' she'd git to that in her own sweet time. However, the second day in Desperation she asks me if Ah was game fer uh "little walk."

"Sure," Ah says, hopin' it was littler than our "little trek."

"OK. You're uh big fella, just about his size, so maybe your feet are too."

"Not sure Ah git yer drift, Miss Dale."

She laughed. Boy! It's kinda like some tinkley little Christmas bells when she laughs. "What I mean is, you can probably fit Dad's bunnies . . . his boots . . . our little walk? Depending on how you hold up . . . maybe a couple of days . . . hope you can lug a fifty pound knapsack."

Well, as they say, it weren't no "walk in the park," an it was gittin late on the second day traipsin' up mountain sides and jumpin' across little rivulets, when Dale stops and slips off her backpack. Ah dropped mine too, as mah shoulders didn't need no encouragin' t' do likewise.

"We're here. We'll make a more permanent camp than last night," says Dale, "might even find some gold for you . . . just kidding, every speck of gold's been cleaned out of these hills long ago. . . . Of course, if we get a real gully-washer in the spring . . ."

"To tell the truth, Dale, Ahm more interested in what you kin tell me about your Daddy and why he sent mah Aunt such uh big bear, than gold."

Well, it were Dales turn t' gimme that durn wonderin' look, but her eyes was soft as duckling down, an' she says some durn thing I didn't understand.

"Maybe it's me whose found gold."

63

WHO OR WHAT

"We've got another hour or so to hike," says Dale.

That warn't uh very good answer to my question, "Why did ya bring me out here?"

"If it ain't where we're goin', why did we camp here?"

"So nobody can say we're connected to where we're going . . . that, and this place is special to me . . . parents actually met here, according to Dad, this exact place."

"An' are we connected to where we're going?"

"You betcha . . . plenty."

"Boy, that sounds like 'home' . . . Minni Soota. "

"One of Dad's favorites, even when he couldn't remember why he spoke like he did . . . don't think 'yes' was in his vocabulary, was kind of a tie . . . between 'you betcha' and 'yeah sure' . . . suppose I shouldn't leave out 'oh yeah.' "

"That's New Boonies talkin', fer sure . . . but . . . but maybe ya could gimme just a little inkle on . . ."

Christmas bells again. "I'm taking advantage of your patience, Mudge. Let's have another cup of tea, and I'll do some explaining." She got up, took the little aluminum pail offen the fire and filled my cup.

I was leaning' up against uh log an' feelin' pretty comfortable; some sorta jay birdie scolded at us, insults I s'pose, fer bustin' inta his peaceful patch of woods, but the little stream, just uh stones throw away, purred like uh contented pussycat. Ah was all ready fer some X-plainin'.

"For most of my life with Dad, you might say he wasn't himself. I really didn't know the man, or at least, all of him. If that's confusing, Mudge, I'll start from what he told me of his life here before I was born. And, to complicate his story, I was a married woman when I found out that my father was a different man than circumstances would reveal him too be."

I nodded, but didn't have no clue what she was talkin' about.

"You know that Dad came from the states, your home town, to seek his fortune here . . . mining gold. This spot, right here where we sit, is his original claim."

"Do you own it?"

"Oh goodness no . . . played out, not worth the rent."

"Rent?"

"To the state of Alaska. . . . Most of this land has been fine-tooth combed for gold . . . copper too. I doubt there's a nickel's worth left on this site, outside of what might wash down with the spring melt. Actually, that's why Toby . . . my husband, wanted to leave Desperation. Of course, I just couldn't."

"Ya mind my askin' why?"

"Dad was so stubborn, but he needed some looking after . . . was never one-hundred percent after the attack."

"I meant, yer husband . . . left on account . . ."

"Oh. Toby was ambitious. When he decided there really wasn't any gold here, he wanted to try his hand with salmon . . . worked on a fishing boat so he could earn a stake . . . buy his own boat, but that's not the way it went. He and I were pretty well kaput by then, but still, I was very saddened when he was lost."

"Lost?"

"The whole crew . . . storm . . . it happens."

Well, I don't wish no other fella that kinda luck but, on the other hand, mah heart come stomping back from somewheres south of Oregon, tellin' me we could git goin' "forward" again.

"Ah am sorry fer yer loss, Dale, but ya do sound recovered."

The wonderful laugh, again. "Oh I'm recovered alright."

"That's good, an' you was sayin' yer Daddy got hisself attacked?"

"Right over by that little creek, if he got mother's description accurately . . . which might or might not be . . ."

"Who done it?"

"Not who, exactly. What."

64

Good er Bad Kin Be Shocking

Dale leaned back an' kinda dreamy-like stared down t' the little creek. I leaned forward, wantin' t' know "what" attacked her Daddy. "Well, what was it," Ah asked?

"According to Dad, who didn't remember anything about the attack, it was a grizzly."

"Just uh minute, is it me er what? Somethin' just don't add up here."

"It'll add up for you, Mudge, I hope. I guess my father was digging into the stream bank. I don't think he knew it, but mother was gathering berries on the far side of that little rise, right there." She pointed to a bump in the hillside, or mountainside, depending on how far ya seen it from. "She heard a great commotion and snarling . . . and screams. She peeked over the edge of that hillock and saw a bear mauling Dad.

"He was limp and bleeding from a terrible head wound, and she thought he must be dead. Maybe the bear thought so too, because it evidently lost interest and simply wandered off. When Mother found that the man was still alive, though '*baldzaey lggeyi*,' that's 'white as the moon,' in Ahtna, she went to get help.

"Dad was taken back to their encampment and mother nursed him while he healed. He recovered physically, but remembered nothing about the attack or from his past, except two words, which everyone just assumed were names, Windsong, and the name he eventually gave me, Thudalia. He could never explain why he chose that name for me, until after the robbery."

"Lemme git this straight. Yer Mama an' Daddy come out here fer gold diggin' an' pickin' berries. . . ."

"Yes, but no. Dad was working his gold claim. Mom came from the encampment . . . she was Ahtna. . . ."

I suppose I looked sorta flummoxed. "What's uh Ahtna?"

"Men and women indigenous to this area . . . from the Ahtna Tribe. Indians!"

I could see she was uh mite impatient. "Ahm sorry, Dale, Ah just didn't know."

"Oh, I'm sorry too, Mudge. Please . . . didn't mean to be . . . sharp." She reached out and put her hand on mine.

Wowie! I don't s'pose there was electricity fer uh hundred miles, excepting the shock what run up mah arm and down t' mah . . . well, just down.

"Dad's Ahtna name was Fights with Bear; he stayed with my mother and her people, I think for a couple of years, and might . . . have worked his claim here. They were finally joined in our . . . tradition. . . . Funny, when I say our, I mean Ahtna. Finally, Dad and Mother moved to Desperation. Actually, they were expelled from the tribe."

"The Indians was prejudiced on yer Daddy?"

"Please don't say 'Indians' like that, Mudge. I'm as much Indian as so-called White. Like Dad told me after the robbery, he was a descendant of Kentucky mountain folks, and their ancestry 'might have been cave-men and monkeys.' But we can get to that later. For now, this is the short explanation of why Mother and Dad settled in Desperation . . . and, eventually, as much as I know, or can piece together, about your bear. . . . Incidentally, among the herd of Dad's stuffed animals, the mate to your bear is back home and . . ."

"What . . ." Ah was gonna ask her what she meant by 'mate' but she held up uh hand an' I just let her go on.

"Over time, some men in the encampment thought Dad's memory loss was due to evil spirits, and led by an important hunter, they tried to drive the spirits out of Dad . . . beat him nearly . . . they nearly accomplished what the bear started. I guess my mother was a very unusual woman; she stabbed that hunter, ringleader . . . in the heart, and the Elder's Council punishment was expulsion."

"Boy! Ah'd say 'unusual' were uh pretty good guess!"

"You're right on the guessing, Mudge. . . . I never knew her."

Never knowed her? Even the little stream gurgled like laughin' at such uh tale. "What? Ya funnin' me on this story?"

The way Dale threw the leavin's outta her cup, I knowed she was mad. She stood up and says, "Let's go . . . and for the record . . . was in my letter, I didn't know Mother because she died giving birth . . . to me."

Oh, dammies! Ah put mah foot right inta mah mouth. "Ahm really sorry, Dale, it's kinda complicated fer me t' understand good."

"It is complicated, Mudge, but what you absolutely have to understand is that it's a truthful story. I sense that you're a 'man-of-his-word.' " She patted her chest. "I'm a 'woman-of- mine'!"

We walked without talkin' fer quite uh spell an' finally come t' uh open spot in the tall trees, the size of half uh city block. There was uh fair amount of junky stuff lyin' around, like old poles, an' boxes, an' such. Uh hawk was sittin' on the rusty runners of uh crumblin', overturned dogsled an' flapped away with uh scream. All the stuff was overgrowed with grass an' half-growed trees an' such, an' it was no trick t' see that folks had lived here, but the place musta been deserted fer years.

Dale swept her arm in an circle, indicating the clearing. She spoke softly. "My mother's hometown . . . equivalent to your New Boonies."

65

SPARKS

"We'll just rest here a while, Mudge." I notice her voice is just above uh whisper.

We sat on a blowed over tree trunk, but Dale was doin' lots more lookin' around than resting. She didn't say uh word, so I didn't say nothing either. We musta set there for twenty minutes er so, just listening to the wind gittin cut t' pieces on the jagged edges of spruce an' cedar. There was a far-away sound like somebody stomped on the ground an' Dale whispers, "Moose." Finally she gits up an' says, "Can't be too careful . . . it's OK to go."

Dale waded inta uh tangle of tall grass an' weeds what was sort of uh struggle t' git through.

"Don't follow me, Mudge. Walk beside me, but about ten feet over . . . want to leave little trail as possible . . . I take a different way in and out of here every time."

"On account of bears?"

She gives uh little laugh. "Only if they're 'Smokey' bears."

Ah couldn't imagine what she was meanin' so I didn't say nothing. Then Ah understood, on account of she took uh good look around an' bent over, pullin' uh buncha dead branches offen a couple of sheets of corrugated steel roofing what was crusty with rust an' dirt. Under them was uh small pit with uh long-nosed copper kettle an' gear what

Ah seen uh dozen times in New Boonies: stuff fer uh still. "You makin'?"

"That's right, Mudge . . . the 'shine you had in your tea this morning . . . don't do much, it's strictly a winter project, so I can move the stuff . . . sled. It's mostly just for neighbors. . . . Thought about giving it up, but . . . it's . . . kind of linked with Dad . . . all those years, he made lightning right here."

Mah guess is, some of them "neighbors" might not be close enough t' hear uh cannon go off in Desperation.

"This and taxidermy were Dad's main interests . . . until the robbery . . . though he never gave up chasing gold . . . was the gold that sent me to the fancy California school."

"Mah Uncle's gonna do perfssorin' in California. . . . Ah never been there."

"I didn't much like it, went to please Dad. Got a few rough edges knocked off . . . enough insults to last me forever."

"Why was . . ."

"Too many of my 'colleagues' thought 'half-breed' was incompatible with making the Dean's List. Came home . . . never finished. . . . Everything looks fine here." She carefully recovered and concealed the pit, then glanced up at the overcast-dimmed sun. "Getting late, let's get back."

"Why'd we come all the way out here? Ya coulda just told me bout it."

"It didn't hurt you to see it, Mudge. . . . Dad loved this place so. Even after the robbery, for the brief time that he lived, he spoke lovingly about it. I already told you he made me bring him out here. . . ." She hesitated, then said, "Maybe I'm just waiting for somebody to talk me out of this . . . business . . . foolishness." She looked right at me, but kinda broke the spell by sayin', ". . . Might be the last time I visit Mother's village."

Neither of us said uh word as we tramped back t' where we was campin'. Supper was jerky an' willow tea – plain.

The sun had just took uh break inta uh gloomy sky, an' uh evening chill brung us close t' the fire, what had burned down t' uh glowin', gray mound. Dale stirred it with uh stick, sendin' uh thousand little temporary sparks leaping outta the coals, riding the heat, up into the treetops. It reminded me of the moths that used t' dance in the movie projector's beam on summer Saturday nights in New Boonies; it gimme uh kinda stopped-up feeling in mah throat as I was slidin' inta mah sleepin' bag.

Guess if Ahm gonna find out about Old Bruin, Ah better keep askin'. "You've mentioned uh robbery quite uh few times . . . like it was pretty durn important. . . ."

"Important! It sure as hell was . . . it's why you're here now . . . started the whole darn thing, made Dad send one of his precious bears to your Aunt. . . . Sorry, got kind of carried away. I'm . . . I've . . . not forgotten that your whole purpose up here is find out why Dad sent the grizzly to her. That bear had been a fixture in the bar for . . . I don't know, forever . . . and I'm curious too. Maybe we can figure it out together . . . but I need to tell Dad's story in the order of . . . of the . . . way . . . I think he lived it. But no more tonight, Mudge, OK?"

Ah could tell she was wrasslin' with some pretty strong feelin's so I closed mah bag an' mah eyes.

Was cold, but the sleepin' bag was nice an' warm. Air was still an' quiet except fer an occasional bird er somethin' peepin', an' now an' then uh little snap from the dyin' fire. And for the first time, I noticed uh smell of spruce an' cedar, kinda strong, actually . . . was the last thing on mah mind an' just about t' sleep when Dale asks if Ahm awake.

". . . You're right, Mudge, I should have just tried to explain everything back home. Thought this might give you some feel for . . ." She paused and coughed, I think to cover up uh sob. ". . . No, damn it! There's no other way to say it, I dragged you along on my personal pilgrimage because I wanted your company . . . wanted to mix you up with . . ." She didn't finish her sentence, but reached over an' tapped the bag over mah shoulder.

219

"I ain't got nobody I'd . . . I'd rather give company to."

"Good night, Mudge."

Now I knowed how them little sparks felt, sailin' up into the night.

66

EAT, DRINK, & BE-HAVE

We got back t' Desperation, an' Dale fixed up uh moose-meat dinner with mashed potatoes, wild onions, an' some little blue berries that she said the bears especially like. Uh rhubarb pie an' real coffee finished off stuffin' me.

"How ya git potatoes an' stuff t' grow up here?"

"Well, let's see, I have a dozen or so half whisky barrels sitting out back that the potatoes do just fine in, the rhubarb too. As for the "stuff," the moose come right up t' my door and ask to be shot, same with the wild onions, except that you have to be careful of those guys, some wild onion "stuff" looks just like it . . . deadly poisonous. The berries are a little different, I have t' beat off the bears with a club to get a little privacy when berry picking."

Dale smiled, but Ah really couldn't tell if she were happy-funnin' me, er what. She gotta pretty sharp mind with uh tongue t' match. Ahm sorta gittin' the reason fer her kinda complicated story about her Dad; she goes in fer X-plainin' stuff down t' that last nut an' bolt . . . er berry.

"Why Ah asked is, it's uh lotta work t' raise potatoes in New Boonies, so Ah kin appreciate it must be tough up here."

"Speaking of 'tough,' you hold up well under fire, Mudge. Sarcasm is a specialty . . . should probably say shortcoming, of mine."

"Gee Miss Thudalia, Ah wouldn't exactly say . . ."

"And yours is acting like a dumbbell, which I know damn well you're not."

"Well, Ah . . ."

"Just quit your bumbling for a minute, and come into my bedroom, Mudge."

Ah didn't know what t' think, but it were uh invitation Ah warn't gonna do uh lotta extra thinkin' on.

67

Is You Is or Is You Ain't uh Tough Guy?

It were uh ordinary bedroom except for just one thing, standin' in uh corner was uh brown bear goin' all the way up t' the ceiling. It were uh dead ringer fer the bear what Lawyer Thudmunson was keepin' fer me.

"It's almost a perfect match to yours, Mudge . . . which was a fixture in the bar." She sorta rubbed one of the bruin's outstretched paws. "Look at those claws . . . big as my fingers. Imagine my Dad getting swiped with one of these. That would wipe out most any memory. . . . Lucky he had a head left."

"Ah see. . . ."

"He loved his stuffed critters, especially the grizzlies. What I don't see, and I suppose part of what you want to know, is why he was so darn insistent on sending the other one to his old . . . old what . . . love?"

"The lady you was named after sure seemed t' think they loved each other."

"Oh, I don't dispute that, not after what he said, almost the moment he got his memory back.

It just . . . just sort of negates my mother . . . what she went through with him. But, of course, that certainly wasn't his fault . . . her choice, actually, she must have been a tough woman."

"You don't seem t' be no sissy, neither."

"Why do say that, Mudge?"

"Well, fer one thing, ya kin tucker me plum inta the ground on uh two day hike, an' fer another, instead of hangin' uh picture of daisies on yer wall there, ya got uh billy club. . . . That ain't tough?"

Dale give her kinda sweet giggle, which didn't sound tough at all. "That's not a billy club, even though it was used as one. . . . Dad really wanted to hang on to the darn thing. . . . I just haven't had the heart to throw it out."

"OK then, if I ain't uh 'dumbbell,' how come you always seem t' be talking circles around me? It ain't uh billy, but 'it was used as one.' Ya would like t' throw it away but ya keepin' it. See what Ahm gittin' at . . . things ain't but they is, an' they is, but they ain't. Guess Ahm just too simple t' keep up with ya."

"Life just isn't simple, Mudge. The robbers hit Dad on the head with this." She grabbed it off the wall hooks that supported each end, an' made uh swipe at mah head. "That's the billy club part. Now, look at it up close. . . ." She handed me the nearly foot an' uh half long club. ". . . You can see it's a bone, actually the femur from a grizzly."

"Oh, Ah . . ."

"Let me finish . . . Dad wanted to keep it because it brought his memory back . . . day or so after the attack. He said it made him Johnny Windsong again. You know, almost the very first thing he did was get into Anchorage where he met with an attorney, who contacted the lawyer in Huns Point, and then he got Gears to build a cabinet for the bear that he sent down to you folks. It seemed like demons driving him to get that done." She took the bone from me and replaced it on the wall.

"We went to Anchorage together, to make sure the shippers got that monster crate on the plane OK. It must have cost a couple of king's ransoms to send it, but Dad was happy. It was when we came back home that he told me about suspecting the "bad guys" all along.

224

68

Luck Cuts Both Ways

"Dad said that for over a year, he'd suspected that the two good-for-nothings, bumbling fools actually, who came up here, might try a robbery. Remember, he thought he was Fights with Bear, and so did everybody else, right up until he was injured . . . in the botched robbery."

"He knew about it in advance?"

"At the time, he suspected . . . maybe . . . no, I think he was certain it was the two characters who worked in the Atlas Warehouse . . . in Anchorage . . . where for years he'd picked up his taxidermy supplies ordered from Outside. They'd seen him paying freight charges, and figured he had a stash of gold up here that was worth stealing. . . ."

"Why would . . . ?"

". . . Coming to that. Dad was quite well known . . . proprietor of the Big Nugget Saloon and by his Indian name, Fights with Bear, which carried an . . . aura, no, not quite the right word . . . mystique maybe, something like the cowboy image of a stateside bull-rider . . . how many guys are tough enough to survive a bear attack? A lot of folks thought he was rich, especially because he paid for everything with gold. He'd shave off a sliver from the little nuggets he always carried and . . ."

"He carried nuggets around?"

"He never quit prospecting, and like most of the old gold grubbers around here, he was pathologically secretive about any find, but

. . . when it came to paying for something, he was . . . it wasn't at all unusual for miners to pay in dust or shavings. I've had plenty of old Sourdoughs pay for drinks with gold and set a poke of dust on the bar that might have been worth thousands. I remember him coming back from town and saying, 'They were watching, again. . . . They might of followed, maybe all the way here.' " He made me get holstered up, right on the spot. Of course, I didn't want to . . . the S & W's heavy. But then . . . it's a long story."

"What's uh S & W?"

"Revolver . . . Smith and Wesson. You don't have them stateside?"

"Well, I s'pose, but Ah ain't never been much of uh gun guy. . . . What's the long story, kin ya try uh short one?"

"OK. I'll make it short, for now, but it deserves all the details. It's a story of luck; Dad was lucky to get himself back, if only temporarily, and I was lucky that I was wearing my hardware. I was right here in my bedroom when I heard the scuffle. . . . Dad yelled and I ran out to the bar just as a fellow grabbed the bear femur, that one. . . ." She pointed to the clubby looking bone she'd put back on the wall. ". . . Dad was always fiddling with some darn animal bones, for his taxidermy stuff. Anyway, it was lying on the bar and this guy grabs it and hits Dad with a vicious swipe of the thing, right alongside of his head; Dad fell like a stone off a cliff. The SOB raised the bone again, this time at me, and I dropped him with a couple of shots into his thigh. His partner came racing in the front door with a double-barrel leveled at me, and I just emptied the cylinder into him. . . . Sheriff said he was probably dead before he hit the floor. I was lucky to have survived. . . . Worst luck in my life, to have lost Dad. But that was far from the end of it. . . . When Dad revived, and it took a couple of days, he was still Fights with Bear but he was also a man I'd never met, Johnny Windsong."

69

LOSING & FINDING

Dale pats the bed an' gimme uh wink. She says, "We stay any longer in here, I'll demand a marriage proposal . . . besides, I could go for a cup of tea."

Well, Ah didn't say nothin', but Ah didn't think stayin' longer in her bedroom would uh been so bad. Proposin' might take some thinkin' on . . . but maybe it warn't such uh bad idea neither. But we went out t' the bar an' Dale lights the little propane burner fer tea water; it's just the size of uh single burner what's on mah stove at home.

She fetched out a kerosene pail from behind the bar, an' filled the three Coleman double-mantle lanterns what give off uh nice yellowish-white light an' uh slight hiss, sorta like uh gentle wind through high grass. "Dad used to say, 'Never give the customers too much light. If they see who their drinking with, they're liable to leave.' "

"Well, you ain't left yet . . . an' ya seen me in the sunlight . . . that's uh good sign."

"Don't get overconfident, I'm still making up my mind on you, Mudge . . . and that's a semi-serious statement." She smiled out loud with her durn sweet little laugh and poured hot water inta mah cup. "You want a little bracer in there?"

"No thanks, Ah gotta have uh clear head t' deal with you . . . an' that's uh 'semi-serious statement.'" Dale just stared at me so Ah went on.

"Trouble is, Ah don't think mah head has figured out just how much semi and how much serious I oughta be usin' with you."

"You've got a way with words, Mudge, I just can't figure out which way."

We both bust out laughin'. Usin' uh word Frederick taught me, I said, "Maybe we should both be touché ing."

"Not at all, Mudge dear, I'll give you this round hands down. I lose."

Ohmahgosh! "Mudge dear."

"Thudalia, Ah think Ah mighta lost somethin' too." *Like some uh mah heart.*

It's funny, but we had us uh pretty awkward spell, just settin' and sippin' tea an' then Dale says, "Maybe we can find something about your bear in Dad's shed. That's where he did all his taxidermy."

———————◆———————

Shed don't sound very highfalutin', but Johnny Windsong's work spot was uh shed only on the outside: old, gray-as-uh-mouse clapboards an' moss covered roof, but uh dream on the inside. Uh cast iron woodstove, along with uh goodly supply of kindling, sat near the end of the little building. ow in the world it ever got moved to this middle-of-nowhere is plum uh mystery. The rest of the short wall was took up by a couple of wooden cabinets. Ah opened up one of the cabinets; the top shelf held uh row of wore-out lookin' books an' catalogues, the rest was filled with uh buncha funny shaped boards, some rough and some even varnished. "What er these things for?"

"Those are called 'panels,' " says Dale, "deer heads, fish. . . . Most mounts are fixed to a decorative plaque, a panel. . . . There must be a dozen different styles behind the heads in the bar, take a look when we go back. Dad tried to teach me . . . fairly good money in it . . . trophies for tourist hunters, but I really didn't like fiddling with dead animals. And, of course, it helps if you're sort of an artist, which I'm not."

A good sized toothy skull, whiter than uh sheet off uh ghost, give uh spooky smile from one of two waist-high worktables backed to the wall. There was uh treadle powered table saw an' wood-lathe, an' hangin' over by the skull, uh set of hand augers that musta come offen the Mayflower. In fact, all the other fifty er so tools looked t' be plenty old-fashioned; they was all neatly arranged on the walls behind the work benches. The only thing hangin' there, that wasn't uh tool, was uh gunny sack holdin' somethin' lumpy, about the size of uh basketball. Ah'd say it were uh workshop uh lotta guys would kill fer.

Not somethin' ya would expect t' find in uh ordinary workshop was the wall what had uh buncha pigeon holes of various sizes, an' in them holes was uh collection of bones like I never seen before. Each bin had uh little paper what said the kind of bone it held. There was moose, elk, deer, beaver, bear, fox, lynx, wolf, swan, eagle, lots of ducks an' small mammals.

"Wowee, them bones woulda made quite uh zoo . . . when they was alive."

"You must be clairvoyant, Mudge. That's exactly what Dad called them, 'my zoo.' "

"Hey! Lookie here, there's some bones like on yer bedroom wall." I pulled one out an tapped its sorta rounded end on a work bench. "That sure would make uh fair shillelagh."

"A what?" asked Dale.

"Uh shillelagh . . . sort of an Irish back-scratcher, used more often to scratch folks' noggins. How did Mr. Windsong ever git inta stuffin' things . . . do ya know?"

"Matter of fact, I do. Dad said he traded 'a couple of small nuggets' for the saloon. Was owned by Sam Sayagain, who, at the time, was likely the only taxidermist anyone in this neck of the woods had ever heard of. That was probably more than forty years ago now. I guess Mr. Sayagain stuck around for a while and taught Dad "taxidermying," as well as the saloon business . . . while learning prospecting tricks from Dad."

I still had the femur in my hand, an' was sorta idly rappin' the end of it into the palm of my other hand. Boy, no wonder them grizzly bears is so fearsome. I couldn't believe uh bone could be this heavy, sure as heck was heaver than the one on Dale's bedroom wall; this one musta been an old fella. Then I noticed some little scratches in the side of the bone. "Well, I'll be hornswoggled," I says, "these here lines look a lot like the ones on the door t' mah bear down in Huns Point."

"What's that?" asks Dale.

"Right there, on the side . . . them little scratches, there." I held the bone fer Dale an' pointed to uh buncha grooves what looked sorta like the grooves in the door t' the big case holdin' mah bear.

"That looks like the Roman numeral eight, Mudge . . . and look at this." She pointed at more scratches, what was really hard t' see. "It's really faint, but that looks like an Arabic number . . . ah, not sure, could be . . . sixty-four, following the numeral."

Ah squinted real hard, but Ah still couldn't make it out. Ah give the bone t' Dale an' said, "This is just about like the bone on yer wall, but seems uh heck of uh lot more stout."

She hefted the femur, then laid it on uh workbench an' picked it up again. "You're right, Mudge. I think this is quite a bit heavier."

"The one on yer wall, it got these little lines?" Ah asked.

"I really don't know . . . don't think I ever looked that closely at it. Let's go take a look. . . . Bring that heavy one along."

The bone what Dale kept on her bedroom wall was smooth all over. It was ordinary as could be except fer uh hole driller inta the big end. Ah was sittin' at the bar an' pulled over the Coleman what shined a really bright light on it; for sure, there wasn't no mark anywheres on it. The heavy femur was layin' on the bar, its big end toward the lantern, an' that was when Ah spotted uh faint little circle in the top of the bone. Thought it might be mah imagination but when Ah held it close up t' the light, it sure looked like uh sorta plug of some kind. Dale was behind the bar, cookin' up some chili an Ah asked her if she'd come around t' the front on account of she might git hurt back there.

"What on earth do you mean . . . how can I get . . . ?"

"Am gonna try an' X-perry-mint . . . an t' be truthful, Ah got kinda uh bum record with X-perry-mintin'. . . . You mind if I bust this bone up uh little?"

"Why would you do that, Mudge?" But she came an sat on uh stool.

"On account of I wanna see what's makin' this old bone so heavy." I raised it up an give it uh fine, smart whack onta the bar an' the end of the dried-out bone shatters inta uh thousand pieces . . . all except what was stickin' outta the bottom part in mah hand. About as thick as mah finger, it looked like uh sorta wire what reflected the Coleman lantern's light in uh color remindin' me of uh glass of fresh poured Leinenkugel. On second thought, the color was uh dead ringer fer the yolks on them sunny-side-ups, Dale made fer breakfast this mornin'.

70

All That's Gold Don't Have t' Glitter

Dale didn't say nothing, just reached out t' me; I put the thing in her hand. She holds on t' the bone part like the coppery-lookin' wire might bite er somethin', but then, with her other hand, wiggles the wire a little, freein' it t' come out. She lays it on her palm and moves her hand up and down, feelin' its heft. "My god, Mudge, you know what this is?"

"Fer sure, it ain't part of the critter's O-riginal equipment."

"Ya darn tootin' it 'ain't'! . . . oh, now you've got me speaking 'Mudge'." The scale set was sitting on the end of the bar an' she pulled it over and put the wire into one of the pans. When she finished puttin' little weights in the other pan she says, "That's just about twenty-one ounces, on the nose . . . at close to $500 . . . that figures to be somewhere around ten grand!"

"Assumin' it's what you're hopin' but ain't even said yet."

"Seen dust and nuggets all my life, what do you think this is?" she lifted the nugget she wears as a necklace . . . "Mudge, I – know – gold!"

"Ah am real happy fer yer good fortune, Dale, Ah really mean it."

"What do you mean, my good fortune?" She grabs me off the bar stool and dances me around till Ah though we was gonna tip over from dizziness. "It's ours, Mudge . . . it's ours, it's ours!"

When we finally set back down, I was plum winded. Dale was bubbly-like laughin' an' X-sighted, but Ah was gittin' hungry.

"Lets go look at Dad's zoo. We'll be like prospectors . . . without the agony!"

"Don't know about you, Dale, but Ah think Ah could do prospectin' better on uh stomach that ain't complainin' and uh night's sleep."

"Not going to argue with the prospector-in-chief. Most of those bones . . . been there for years and one more night won't hurt anything."

———————◆———————

Was sometime in the night Ah woke t' what Ah thought were uh faraway wolf howlin' er maybe uh owl callin' but was actually the floorboards squeekin'. Dale come inta mah room an set on the edge of the bed. She put her hand on mah shoulder, almost rubbin' it, which mighta been wishful thinkin' on mah part.

"You awake, Mudge?" she whispers.

Was Ah ever! "Yes."

"Dad made us partners . . . well, indirectly. You feel like we're partners?"

"Yeaaah." I sure wondered where she was goin'.

"I have to tell you, I was really hurt, hurt and disappointed, when Dad made a stranger . . . as far as I knew then, the Thadalia lady, a partner in the saloon, which turned out to be you. I . . . I was all prepared not to like you, Mudge . . . not you specifically, but whomever. . . ."

"Ah kin understand that. Everbody likes t' make their own choices."

"It's not because you found gold in that bone . . . just wanted you to know that I think you're as good a partner . . . as a person could have. . . . Hope you like our partnership." She got up and left before I got my thinking-cap on t' reply. But Ah coulda told her Ah though our partnership were good as gold.

71

OUTHOUSE EPIPHANY

Couldn't tell by the light out what time it was, an' Ah hadn't bothered t' wind mah watch once since puttin' down uh foot in Desperation. No matter, Ah pulled on mah clothes and made uh visit t' the little house settin' backa the taxidermy shed. It warn't just uh outhouse, it were uh way-out house; Ah shoulda put on boots on account of mah feet near froze off gittin' there, an' didn't git no warmer while I was settin' there. Still, it were uh good time fer thinkin', an' I needed t' think on why Dale's Daddy sent Aunt Thudalia uh bear.

He was big on stuffin', that's fer sure. . . . Durn deer head starin' down at me settin' here proves that. . . . Course, he also give her half of the Big Nugget Saloon. . . . Sure ain't worth much. . . . S'pose it's got some value . . . valuable! Ohmahgosh! Could that be it?

Ah must of smithereened all the speed records fer uh feller gittin' his pants up in uh outhouse. Ah run back t' the saloon an' plum busted inta Dale's bedroom.

"Wake up Dale! Wake up! Ah need to know . . ."

"Wha . . . what do mean barging into my bedroom . . . you gone crazy?"

"Ah need t' know . . ."

"What you're gonna need is a fancy barber and a good plastic surgeon, if I decide to part your hair with this club." She reaches over an' grabs the bone offfen the wall, next t' the bed.

Wowee! Ah'd say she were uh plum distractin' sight. But Ah was thinkin' way too hard about bears an' bones t' let distractin' git inta mah head. "Say, fer uh gal what come inta mah bedroom with no invite, you're bein' mighty snippy, Miss Thudalia."

She calmed down an' said, "I suppose I am being a little theatrical . . . no pajamas does that. Matter of fact, I'm more comfortable with you waking me up than you might imagine."

"Any other time an' I'd sorta follow up on that line of thought . . . but right now, I gotta know exactly what your Daddy said . . . his last words. . . . Kin ya remember um . . . exactly?"

"Of course, just like I told you, 'No nugget, no nugget . . . golden bear.' It's why I repainted the saloon sign . . . but let's get to our little prospecting venture. I want to see those other bones. Please get out of here and let me get dressed."

"Maybe the prospecting is closer than ya thinks. Didn't ya say your bear here is the same as I got?"

"He did both of them when I was just a kid . . . been around here forever."

"You mind if I open your bear here up, sorta un stuff 'im?"

"You are crazy! Why would you do that?"

"T' see if there's somethin' . . . an' maybe I got somethin' in mah bear."

"And I had hopes for you . . . Every once in a while I used to help Dad carry this old bear out to the shed . . . he put something on the fur, to keep pests away and just generally freshen it up . . . Mr. Bear is my friend . . . and you want to tear him apart? I don't think so."

"Please, Dalia, it might solve uh lotta questions. We kin be real careful . . . did you ever see how your Daddy did his freshening?"

"No. What the devil does that have to do with wanting to open it?"

"Listen to me, Dalia, 'no nuggets, no nuggets,' an' you've said yerself, he had lots of nuggets . . . golden bear . . . listen t' me careful now, gold – in – bear. Ah think yer Daddy mighta been tellin' you there was gold – in yer bear."

72

CRAZY AS UH . . . CRAFTY, TOO

"Gold in Mr. Bear? That's about the nuttiest thing I ever heard. Mudge, I swear, you touch one hair on Mr. Bear, and I'll give you a demonstration of what we do to outlanders that get out of hand. . . . It'll be six shots, and I won't be pouring um at the bar! I mean it, get out of here! And don't ever come in here again!"

Boy! Had Ah ever struck uh nerve er somethin'. She was practically screamin' by the time she finished up. Well it don't take no house t' fall on me to know where I ain't wanted. Ah skedaddled outta her bedroom, went inta mine, throwed my stuff inta mah duffle bag, and went over to see Kincaid. Asked him if Ah could arrange with somebody t' git me back t' Anchorage in uh hurry.

"Yer in luck, boy, was gonna go myself, next week, need new dog traces . . . Government buys um for me, ya know, mail delivery an' all, an besides, gotta tooth bittin' at my mouth like uh cornered mink, but now's as good as next week. . . ." Kincaid spit uh chaw of tobacco inta uh bucket of sand, which looked like it had seen uh fair bit of spittin'. He put a forefinger inta his mouth an' kinda gingerly felt around his teeth, fer the hurtin' one Ah suppose, then he says, "Matter uh fact, I think today's lots better'n next week."

Kincaid was every bit as spry as Dale when it come t' handlin' uh dog team. Of course, Ah got t' ride in the sled. Did some walkin' though, on account of in places, the snow was spotty.

Kincaid said it were the earliest good-weather Spring they'd had, that he could remember.

———————◆———————

Mini Tropolis was cold an' overcast, nothin' new there; the robins, just returned from their southern vacation, seemed willin' t' just set an' wait till Mama Nature got around t' warmin' things up before prospecting for worms on the front lawn. Sorta matched my mood. Fer awhile, up North there, I had been thinkin' of writin' a letter down t' Mr. Foreman, t' tell him Ah was stayin' up in Alaska . . . really liked Dale, but Ah guess that's goin' nowhere. When Ah got home Ah just set an' stared outta the window. It got dark an' I got t' thinkin' how everybody in mah life what made me happy was gone; Ah was feeling real bad fer mahself when uh light popped on in MerryMae's house. That was kinda strange, she bein' gone, along with Chrys an' Socrates, down t' Jamaica. Went t' the window t' see what Ah could see, an' by golly, there was the fortune-tellin' lady herself.

Well, before ya could say Jack Robinson – woulda sure been better off steerin' clear of mah great, great grandad – Ah was settin' in MerryMae's dinin' room enjoyin' chocolate cake an' egg coffee, baskin' in a regular Alaskan roaring bore-E-Alice of friendship: MerryMae had gimme uh hug what durn near choked me, Socrates squawked his special "hello" squawk, and Chrys pulsed waves of pastel greens an' yellows.

"It ain't just the cake, MerryMae, I can't tell ya how glad Ah am to see all of ya! How long ya back fer?"

"Think we're here to stay."

Wow! Mah heart leaped right up inta mah throat with the chocolate cake!

Socrates hops onta the arm of mah chair; boy, was Ah ever glad t' see 'im so friendly.

MerryMae offers me uh second piece of cake, which Ah took – just t' be polite.

"Settle back, Mudge, we've got a story you can put in your book."

"Ah'd like t' hear yer story, but, t' tell the truth, I ain't thought of writin' uh word lately."

"Maybe our story will get your pen going again. You recall that I got my dream job?"

"Yeah, curin' some sort of memory problems with uh physic."

"That's . . . close, Mudge . . . Curator of Grimoires at the Museum of Metaphysics . . . sort of a special librarian for arcane books of spells and magic . . . wonderfully educational."

"Didja git educated on how t' spell magic OK?"

"Oh, better than that. I learned a raft of new incantations and conjurations. . . . Even startled Chrys one evening, when I called up a spirit cloud of sunlight. But, I had one little problem. One day, I worked so hard invoking a necromantic spell, so one of the museum's Directors could talk to his . . . a deceased girlfriend, that the grimoire I was exhorting from overheated and caught fire, and, well, to make a long story short, the museum burned down, consuming the books, texts, scrolls, everything, even the clay tablets with the most ancient curses were ruined. It was terrible. And worse, the Directors, who are all skilled in the black arts, blamed me . . . said it was all due to my carelessness. They wanted to confiscate Chrys . . . claimed he was still a citizen of Jamaica. And they threatened to turn me into a pillar of salt if I didn't leave the country immediately – without Chrys, of course. . . . Was awful, their spies were everywhere!"

"How did ya manage t' git here without gittin' uh . . . salted?"

"Was Socrates. Don't know where he found it, or how he got the idea, but he brought me a bowling bag. I caught on, and smeared black shoe polish all over Chrys . . . told the airport customs guys I had just left a bowling demonstration. They glanced in the bag, assumed Chrys was a small bowling ball and passed me on."

"Don'tcha worry about them Director guys puttin' out a hoodo er somethin' on ya?"

"No. Their curses can't travel further than a vampire bat with a full stomach of blood."

"That's better un anything I could write . . . but maybe I kin try. Gittin' late, thanks fer the cake and the story." I got up t' go and Socrates flaps up t' my shoulder. I looked at MerryMae; she nodded. Chrys give a bright flash of orange and settled down to uh mellow green.

When we entered our house, Socrates says, "The Jamaica adventure was fun, but if it's OK with you, Mudge, this is my home."

73

There's Gold in Them Thar Holes . . . Maybe

We pulled into the parking lot of the Point Professional Building, where Mr. Thudmunson had his office. "We're gonna take uh bear apart, hope you don't find that too grizzly." Socrates just stared at me. "Hey, ain't that funny?"

"I'm trying to figure it out," says Socrates.

"Ya know, bear, grizzly . . . it's uh grizzly bear."

"I was thinking black bear."

"Never mind."

We got the key from Pilfer's secretary and took the freight elevator down to the vault. We entered Mr. Thudmunson's storage area and I closed the door, for privacy. Socrates settles himself on the back of the only chair in the room. As Ah set down mah tool bag, an' unlocked the crate door, Socrates says, "I never let on that I could talk . . . or read. You're the only one I ever told. And, Mudge," he paused, "I'm sorry for taking off with Chrys. He's a great guy, but I left you alone . . . shouldn't have."

"I'm glad you're back, guy . . . an', by the way, I almost fell for a really nice girl . . . Alaska. I was in Alaska while you was in Jamaica." I started feeling the bear for anything out of the ordinary.

"What the heck are you doing?"

"Seeing if anything strange is under the fur, skin actually."

"Like a zeppelin, maybe, or a set of Oxford Dictionaries?

"Actually, gold, Mr. Smarty."

"While you're mining for gold, tell me about Alaska."

"There ain't much t' tell. Aunt Thudalia gotta in heritance from Johnny . . . her old love. . . ."

"Aunt Thudalia . . . ?"

"Yeah, Mom, my adopted Mom, ya know, the lady what gimme the Dieffenbachia, the big green plant you didn't think much of. Anyway the Johnny feller had a daughter what I thought was the nicest little lady Ah ever laid eyes on . . . but she got mad at me fer wantin' t' see if there was gold in her bear."

"Mudge, when you write the great American Novel, I hope you tell a better story. . . . There's more bears than this one?"

"Yeah. Thudalia's got one."

"I thought Thudalia inherited this one?"

"This here bear is Aunt Thudalia's. The girl I fell for up to Alaska is Johnny's daughter; her name is Thudalia too, and Johnny give her a bear, just like this one."

"I can't bear to hear this."

I just stared at Socrates.

"Hey," he says, "that's funny."

"I was thinkin' naked," I says.

"Never mind." He fluffs his feathers, and rearranges himself on the chair back. "Now that we've got our little tit-for-tat joke thing out of the way, I'm going for a nap . . . long ride up here, made me sleepy."

———◆———

Finally took tin snips and cut uh couple dozen holes intah the bear. Nothing. *Gosh*, I thought, *maybe Dale was right*. It wasn't until Ah cut its right foreleg clean off that Ah discovered the letter behind the bear, taped to the back of the big packing case. The envelope was printed with:

To my Thudalia

Naturally, Ah opened it up and read it, as I'm the closest living thing to mah Aunt.

My Dear Thudalia
I meant to come back to you but, not long after I got up here, a bear mauled me pretty good and I couldn't remember nothing but two words. One was my name and the other was Thudalia. A woman found me and nursed me back to life. I didn't know who I was so it was sort of natural to stay with her. We had a daughter, who I love like I love you. Along the way I found a lot of gold and put it in the hind feet of this bear you got and another bear which my daughter has. Got my memory back in an accident about 3 weeks ago which is how come I am writing this letter but I know I ain't going to live for very long. I ~~know~~ can feel the end so what time left I am going to spend ~~missing~~ thinking about you and loving you.
Goodbye dearest Thuddy
John

I left Socrates sleepin', and went up t' Mr. Thudmunson's office. They made me a copy of the letter and we mailed it off to Dale up in Desperation. Fer some reason, Ah felt sorta bad about wreckin' the bear so Ah asked Mr. Thudmunson if he would take care of whatever gold was downstairs. He said he would, so I went an' picked up Socrates and we drove back t' Mini Tropolis.

There was another letter waitin' fer me when we got home. Mrs. Matilda Zimmermann, mah renter up t' New Boonies, is got promoted from secretarian' t' marryin'. She's gonna tie the knot with the Mayor, an' she give me thirty days notice t' move out of Aunt Thudalia's house.

I s'pose Ah should still be happy, on account Ah guessed right on gold in the bear, but fer some durn reason, I just feel down in the dumps.

74

LIFE GOES UP AND LIFE GOES DOWN, BOTH GOOD AND BAD GO 'ROUND AN' 'ROUND.

Was a couple of weeks before I went back to work at Amalgamated Associates. Mr. Foreman gimme uh nice welcome: ". . . Never had as good a watchman as you, Mudge, good to have you back."

"Thank you, Sir." Ah warn't gonna lie an' say Ah was glad t' be back. Ah warn't, but the book in mah head was startin' t' git printin' in it, an' Ah was kinda glad t' be doin' watchin' soz Ah could work on it again. But, even tryin' like the dickins' didn't actually git none of them words writ down on mah notebook. Got t' thinkin' about Uncle Mort and all the good times we had up t' the Town Tavern; nowadays, with Mort gone t' California, Leinenkugels don't seem t' taste so good as they used to.

Socrates is pretty good company but somehow the newspaper stories he gits excited about don't seem as important like before . . . before what . . . what in tarnation was missin' that took all the flavor outta livin'? Ah don't even care about the "considerable four-chune" what Pilpher Thudmunson says I got in Aunt Thudalia's bear . . . my bear.

When mah shift finished up, an' Ah went home, Socrates was

asleep; Ah felt like Robinson Crusoe without no Freddy, er nobody. Ah wish Ah could go back, t' when Mort was marchin' an' Aunt Thudalia was growing all them cuttin's from her Johnny plant an' Leinenkugels tasted special an' . . . an' Miss Smallermann said, ". . . You have to go forward, to find what's at the end of your rainbow."

Was then I woke up, the sun was streamin' intah the front window an I knew I had t' figure a way t' ride that sunbeam intah uh forward frame of mind.

The doorbell rang an' Ah stumbled intah the living room t' answer it. When Ah opened the door, mah sunbeam carried me plum intah the sun, the moon, the milky way, and the whole beautiful cosmos. Suitcase in hand, the dream Ah hadn't known Ah was dreamin' said, "I'm here to make things right."

———————◆———————

"Where we going, Mudge?"

"T' start uh die-nasty, I hope."

"Is that the boob or the serious fella talking?"

"I'm serious, Dalia. We're headed t' uh place what's mighty special t' me, . . . was real special t' the lady you was named after . . . special on account of her an' yer Daddy."

"My god! What a tragedy they never connected." Dalia gimme uh glance that Ahm hopin' means, "Let's not let history repeat itself."

The countryside had changed some since my last visit. Uh square C-ment block building with uh small sign sayin' "Steel Township" had got built along County #40 an' uh fancy, big house sits right out in the middle of uh field, no more than uh couple miles from Highland Corners. The only Burma Shave sign still sorta standin' was so faded that ya had t' already know what it said to make out, "Don't take," but the little grove of popple trees, just off the intersection, was still there. We parked by um, rolled down the windows, an' listened to um rattle in the late Spring breeze. I swear Ah could hear Aunt Thudalia sayin', "Giving my heart . . . giving my heart," which is what Ah already done, but now I'm gonna say it out loud, t' Dalia.

LIFE GOES UP AND LIFE GOES DOWN,
BOTH GOOD AND BAD GO 'ROUND AN' 'ROUND.
OUR TRAVAILS CAN BE A STRAIN, THOUGH
SWEET, IF ENDING WITH A RAINBOW.

FB

Visit Us Online

At the Three Waters Publishing website, you'll find:

- Blanch's reading and book signing schedule;
- Release dates of new books;
- Excerpts and sample chapters;
- Audiobooks; and
- A newsletter to keep you up to date on all that's new.

Visit us now at:

http://threewaterspublishing.com

About Frederick Blanch

Bitten by the writing bug at the tender age of six, Blanch's literary ambitions suffered setbacks from anxious English teachers, hoping to preserve some continuity and/or common comprehension of the language, and interruptions by protracted stints as life insurance salesman (six years), entrepreneur/printer (twenty years), composer (ten years), actor (dabbled for five or six years), beekeeper (ten years), non-profit director – television producer (fifteen years), and a long, long time nature photographer, none of which derailed a stream of short stories, poetry, plays, novels, and commercial writing. In Blanch's own words, "The path to anonymity has not been easy."

More by Frederick Blanch

Last Words: Frederick's Bionary
Beware the Dogs

and, coming soon from Three Waters Publishing:

Mudge's Best Short Stories

CPSIA information can be obtained
at www.ICGtesting.com
Printed in the USA
FFOW01n0418120615
14140FF